T0194747

THE
EXALTER

FREE TO SERVE

MATTHEW McHENRY

WESTBOW
PRESS®
A DIVISION OF THOMAS NELSON
& ZONDERVAN

Scriptures taken from the Holy Bible, New International Version®, NIV®. Copyright © 1973, 1978, 1984, 2011 by Biblica, Inc.™ Used by permission of Zondervan. All rights reserved worldwide. www.zondervan. com The "NIV" and "New International Version" are trademarks registered in the United States Patent and Trademark Office by Biblica, Inc.™

This is a work of fiction. All of the characters, names, incidents, organizations, and dialogue in this novel are either the products of the author's imagination or are used fictitiously.

WestBow Press books may be ordered through booksellers or by contacting:

WestBow Press
A Division of Thomas Nelson & Zondervan
1663 Liberty Drive
Bloomington, IN 47403
www.westbowpress.com
1 (866) 928-1240

ISBN: 978-1-9736-1369-5 (sc)
ISBN: 978-1-9736-1370-1 (hc)
ISBN: 978-1-9736-1368-8 (e)

Library of Congress Control Number: 2018900194

Print information available on the last page.

WestBow Press rev. date: 01/24/2018

Dedication

I would like to dedicate this book to my closest friend, my wife. I was ready to throw in the towel and never write another book again, but with your encouragement, I took your advice, and with God's guidance, I think I made a great read. You are the kind and loving motivator that a man like me absolutely needs. Thank you for being everything that makes you who you are.

I would like to thank the Daily Audio Bible family of listeners, who prayed for me during this tedious editing process. Thank you to Brian and Jill Hardin for their dedication to their ministry and the time they give to all of us listening on the Daily Audio Bible podcast. I would also like to thank the following ministries that helped encourage me and strengthened my faith. Thank you also to those ministries who provide free downloadable podcasts, which I find priceless. In no particular order: Dr. Lester Sumrall LeSEA Ministries, Kenneth Copeland Ministries, In Touch Ministries of Charles Stanley, Ever Increasing Faith Ministries of Dr. K. C. Frederick Price and Fred Jr., Jack Van Impe International Ministries, Jerry Savelle Ministries, Joel Osteen Ministries, Joyce Meyer Ministries, Bill Winston Ministries, Moore Ministries of Keith Moore, Jesse Duplantis Ministries, and T. D. Jakes Ministries.

Chapter 1

Sometime in your near future …

Zeneth put her hands on her hips in a confrontational manner. "Tyrisha, I don't like what this Knower did," she said. "Why would you let him bring you home? What you're doing is forbidden." She raised her eyebrows, looking for an acceptable answer.

Tyrisha had her back turned to her mother. She rolled her eyes and huffed in the same motion. "Nicolai approached me in his car on the day it was storming very badly last week. I was walking home later than usual from service to the Tirian's estate."

Zeneth wasn't going to allow her daughter to be taken from her by force; the penalty could even be execution. The line forming between Zeneth's eyebrows signified that she was at her highest level of anger.

She warned her daughter, "Oh, so now you know his name, do you? Don't talk to him again. You know what happens to Derogates that talk to Knowers. Just being around a Knower is dangerous enough, because we are exposed to the blindness. The blindness will take over, and before you know it, you will be one of them, and they won't ever let you go back."

Tyrisha glared at her mother, took a step toward her, and then turned to walk to her room.

Zeneth knew that Derogates weren't allowed to have communication with Knowers anyway. Who was this Nicolai, she wondered, and what was he thinking? What was he planning? Zeneth could tell from his servitude sticker that he was in the third-class Knower division. Sure, his job was most likely technical and related to computers, which was nothing violent, but this was a dangerous road.

Chapter 2

A man dressed in black walked up to the door of Zeneth's house. He was large in stature, walked slowly with obvious strength, and said sternly, "It's Sunday! Get to the door and give 20 percent to the Exalter right now."

Zeneth's husband, Leviticus, quickly scrambled to the door with a bowl full of money for the offering to the Exalter. The man in black focused on Leviticus, and his hatred for Leviticus burned in his eyes. As always, the Knower dressed in black had a device that counted the money as it dropped into the bag and then emitted a beep.

Oh, the Only, please just let the Knower leave us in peace, Leviticus thought. The Knower was not happy. The offering was lower than the previous month's, and they both knew it.

"Is this what you think of the Exalter? You think you should give less because you have less? Of course it is. You believe in the false god I would not even utter the name of. Your family had better find more work or else more than money will soon be demanded of you." The Knower turned around and muttered, "Pssht … what am I talking about? The insertion will soon be here, and then all of you wretched Derogates will get what you deserve."

Leviticus could feel the Knower wanting to kill him right there and then. What had he said about an insertion? Leviticus didn't know it, but the insertion was an all-knowing device that would be implanted in each human's right hand, Knower or Derogate. It would show their identity, location, and geographical movement patterns, and even give a summary of their general health through monitoring systems. Most of all, the insertion was linked to accounts accessible to Knowers. This meant that with a simple wand, the government could electronically see all someone had done. Either way, they would know your life in a downloadable minute. Leviticus must have gotten it wrong, and he had better just keep it quiet.

Just one week ago, the Exalter had proclaimed himself as the only one to worship. He then appointed Candon Veswalis as the Seer, to be second-in-command. Years earlier, the Seer, then the Census Chief Official, enacted the census of truth for all people to divide those who would accept the Exalter from those who would not. The Seer then gave the name of Derogates to all those who would not pledge allegiance to the Exalter. The areas where the Derogates live are called the black suet villages. They are exactly what they sound like—dark villages spread out all over the regions of every country. The Knowers, who follow the Exalter, purposely made the areas worse than they were. They plowed over all vegetation and trees, and they stripped the grass from the ground. Only one drinking well was dug for the whole community, and everything else that was built by the Derogates required authorization. The roads were mud, and the housing structures were built from wood and mud blackened from the smoke of the villages' fires. The people there are slaves to the Knowers.

Each day, the Derogates must go out and report to the nearest Knower sanitation facility, where they can wash in the showers in these gym locker-style facilities. They must promptly report to their work stations at whatever job they were given. Everything they use is thrown away and burned in a great furnace. Towels, razors, cloths, and even empty soap bottles must be discarded to destroy the unholy contamination in fire. The work is strict, without breaks or sympathy from any Knower. The Derogates work each day, and at the end of each week, they are given rations of food according to their household size. Each Derogate household is given a specific amount of poverty paychecks from the government. At the same time, a tithe is expected from each Derogate household. The only problem is that the Derogates are required to tithe 20 percent back.

The thought of giving back that money as a tithe or buying much-needed supplies or food haunts every Derogate's mind. Many have died for deciding to eat rather than sacrifice to their holy leader. Younger Derogates do not work until they reach the age of six, which has been declared the age of submission. If only the father Derogate works, then a larger ration is given out. If the Derogate has himself, his unholy wife, and his abominable children working, then smaller rations are given out to each family member.

Leviticus lived in one of these black suet villages and had a family of his own. His father had told him forbidden stories of a book all the Derogates would follow. His father, Lamerc, did not even know the name of the book, because it had been outlawed, and it had been too long since anyone dared whisper the name. The book had been outlawed more than a hundred years before, and all known copies were destroyed and tossed into a volcano. In secret, the Derogates worked hard to take parts of each book so that each village would have at least a partial copy. The Knowers didn't check the books well enough to notice whether any pages were missing. Besides, they hated the book so much, they would not even touch it. It would have been considered unholy and detestable to touch the book barehanded.

All those years ago, the Derogates' religion was outlawed. Only one religion, Unitian, was accepted. Only sixty-six years later, the Exalter was born, and he took his place in government at age twelve. He was thought the little savior of the world born in flesh, and he appointed himself a divine ruler when he turned only thirty-one, giving himself all powers to rule the world. He also appointed a relative as the Seer with whom, it is said, he shared his divine power. Their supernatural powers were undeniable. The Seer had performed many miracles.

Once all the unholy books were assembled so many years ago, they were locked deep in a secret vault. One had to wonder why they were kept and not destroyed at that time. The Exalter then had the unholy books taken to active volcanoes, where the burning was globally televised and recorded. The Seer called down fire from the sky. As the books fell into the mouth of the volcano, they were hit by fireballs. The display was complete overkill. Young children cheered for the power of the great Seer and made noises to mimic the fireballs coming down: "Spew, spew!" It was a demonstration of the Exalter's will and power and emphasized that the evil books must be destroyed and all the ways eradicated.

Chapter 3

Nicolai of the third-class Knower division entered his office the same time he did every morning: at ten o'clock sharp. He would leave each day at 1:30 p.m., just the same. Third-class Knowers always worked a full day of three hours, with a lunch break. The Exalter had demanded these things years ago at the beginning of his power. Nicolai headed in with a long stride, standing just over six feet tall and exhibiting his fit frame. He was always very clean-cut and dressed nicely. He cared about how he looked—not for others, but just for himself. He was the kind of guy who got a haircut every week. He looked like ex-military, but he wasn't. His short, trim brown hair, long limbs, and blue eyes created a catchy look. Nicolai noticed right away that something wasn't right. His chair was turned around, facing the window. His shades were pulled open facing the west, as he could see the red clouds in the distance. The chair turned around slowly, and Nicolai couldn't believe his eyes as he saw the crown atop the Exalter's head.

In his peripheral vision, Nicolai saw what he had only seen on halovision: The Exalter's two Terafin guards stood at the Exalter's sides. They were deeply intimidating in appearance. They were taller than any human, had armor, held scepters, and wore red robes draped over their shoulders. Nicolai knelt and kept his face down, terrified.

Somehow, he spat out in a low tone, "Yah, yah, Your Excellence."

The Exalter spoke after several minutes, but it seemed to take forever: "Nicolai, my servant ... no, no, please rise up, and take a seat across from me. You must know how I love you. I am just here to talk, my son."

Nicolai rose from the office floor and could not bring himself to look the Exalter in the eye. After all, he was staring at the one who they say created him in the form of flesh. How could he look at the Exalter as if he were equal? The Exalter was a man of tall stature. His skin was toned slightly, giving him a perfect, suntanned complexion. His eyes were neither blue nor teal. They seemed to pierce right through you. The Exalter was exactly what one might expect—perfect in every way. His facial structure seemed to demand respect, his muscular body instilled fear, and his confidence was overbearing. He always dressed in fine suits with bold-colored ties.

Most impressive of all was the thin crown on his head. Gold and silver were completely outlawed over a century ago, and the Exalter was the only one who wore these metals. He was eccentric, with silver, platinum, and gold ornaments around his wrist and fingers. At least, that is what Nicolai thought, since he had never seen such metals in person but had only read about them or seen them on the Exalter on the halovision.

What was the Exalter doing here anyway? he wondered. Wasn't he supposed to be going to Russia, with a stop in Iran? What prompted this stop so quick that it wasn't being reported on the news to the States?

"Nicolai, why have you shown interest in some defiled Derogate?"

Nervous, out of his mind, and feeling the heat of blood running to his face, Nicolai replied, as quickly as he could, "Your Excellence, I merely offered a ride home to a young girl when the weather was overbearing. I apologize for any breaking of your holy laws. Please ... have mercy on me for my sins."

The Exalter looked to his left as if to be in thought, smiled slowly, blinking both of his eyes slowly, and then turned his head straight forward to stare right into Nicolai's eyes. "Come now, my son. I know you wanted that Derogate to become one of my servants and a fellow Knower. You wanted her to be on of your wives, didn't you? I know your thoughts, Nicolai, don't forget that. I am all-knowing and all-seeing. You knew that I know you want Tyrisha to be one of your body-sharing partners, didn't you? Yes, you admired her and wanted her."

Nicolai knew he had no way of defending himself. "Holy Exalter, you are, of course, correct as always. Please forgive me."

The Exalter smiled again and nodded approvingly. "I will always forgive you, my son, unless you defy me and join the unholy Derogates. However, I am here to tell you that Tyrisha would only bring you trouble and heartache. I want to protect you. Instead, I think you should choose another young girl named Janae. You see, Janae is coincidentally Tyrisha's best friend, and she will go with you, obey you, and please you. However, I know you, my son. You may try to persuade Tyrisha again. My children must make mistakes in order to learn, but you must learn to rely on me and to trust me completely. I am showing you the future and giving you the choice."

Nicolai could not figure out how the Exalter knew all this information. Was someone spying on him? Why was this so seemingly important?

The Exalter continued, in a barely detectable Italian accent, "Despite your attempts, Tyrisha will not choose to be taken in by you. That is when you will give her a choice. Tell her that if she doesn't come with you, you will take Janae, her best friend, into your house. She'll finally break down and do anything you want to protect her friend. Then and only then, Nicolai, will I give you the privilege to obey me with peace or to deny my will with severe consequences. There you have it. I have given you the gift of seeing the future, and the choice is yours. I suggest teaching a lesson to Tyrisha for believing she could go against my will and thinking she could do better than you, one of my children."

Nicolai sat there in the office, in complete awe. He had never seen the Exalter face to face. He couldn't believe the Exalter cared so much about him that he would appear to him and talk with him in the form of a man.

Nicolai answered, "Thank you, Your Grace, for taking time to visit someone so beneath you as me. You always guide me, and I have listened to your guidance. Thank you."

The Exalter slowly stood up and lowered his chin with a straight face, as if to say, "My pleasure," with an additional body language message of "don't cross me." He then walked slowly out of the office as all the other Knowers fell to one knee in respect, worship, and fear. The office workers would most likely give Nicolai some serious respect. He got a personal visit from the holy Exalter himself. It was such big news. The Exalter's two Terafin guards walked side by side with the Exalter, their heavy footsteps thudding. It's not that the Exalter needed protection; it's that the Terafins were something the Exalter said he had in the heavens and also wanted to have in human form.

Nicolai walked to his office window, staring at all the red clouds, and thought about what the Exalter said. He said quietly, "Red skies this morning, huh? Hope the storm isn't for me."

The Exalter exited the office building and got into his luxurious armored vehicle waiting outside. After a short trip to the airport, he boarding his royal airplane. The Seer was awaiting his return for the short stop to Nicolai. The Seer seemed more like a millionaire businessman. He was always calm and reading something with those expensive-looking designer glasses. The Seer was a man of fine taste; he enjoyed fine dining and got absolutely fine treatment from all of his servants.

The Seer stood up in honor. "Holy Exalter, glad to have you back, sir. I take it your advice to Nicolai was well received?"

The Exalter sat down across from the Seer on another lavish leather seat and poured an alcoholic beverage. The Exalter looked around to his staff and ordered, "Leave us."

The staff left, while the Terafin guards remained in the back of the plane, one on the left and one on the right aisle.

"I don't like this," he began. "My agents have reported to me about this Tyrisha Derogate. And I know you understand what I mean when I say my agents. She is protected by the light and out of our reach. I can do nothing either good or bad for her. I am blocked."

The Seer was still on "Another Cup of Joe" and calmly responded as he was reading, "Who cares if she is protected? What can she do? She is only human."

When the Exalter and the Seer were together in private, they would talk like family, but it was a different story in the public eye. The Seer would put on a show as the Exalter's trained dog in full submission. The Exalter raised his lip in a hateful, staring glare the Seer did not see, as he continued reading.

"Don't you get it, you imbecile? During these times, there has never been a Derogate that has been this protected. I couldn't strike her down if I wanted to. She could have the power to make Knowers turn to Derogates. I have been watching her." The Exalter was not pleased with not seeming to know the end of a situation and even more displeased that the Seer didn't understand the ramifications of all this.

The Seer said calmly, "Relax, Laykeun, you are no doubt the most powerful, are you not? No one will turn from Knower to Derogate; that is just silly. Some impoverished and underprivileged dumb girl is of no concern to us."

The plane sped through the air, and the Exalter was still not pleased, even if the Seer was trying to comfort him by speaking on a first-name basis.

Chapter 4

Only a year ago, in a less-luxurious part of the world, Leviticus was talking with his father, Lamere, about their own problems. They spent some time talking about the Derogate changes and the new powers rising. It was obvious that they both deeply missed June. Seeing each other always made them both think of their wife and mother. It would have been easier to accept a natural death, but they both believed the Knowers had done something with June. They must have killed her or taken her into secret slavery. They both just wanted to believe she was no longer living to ease their worry and for her benefit.

June was everything to the both of them, and more to Lamere. When you have nothing, not even possessions, the only thing important to you is the people around you. June had such beautiful light-brown hair, accompanied by brown and amber eyes. She was gentle, and her distinctive voice was soothing. She would ease Leviticus to sleep as a boy while she told stories of the Only. She respected the ways of the Only and honored him in her life.

Neither Leviticus nor Lamere ever forgot the day a level 2 division Knower came to their muddy doorstep at house 252. It wasn't even that long ago, only two months, but it seemed so long. They had asked everyone they could find if anyone saw a woman in any household with the house number 252. No one had known or conveyed that they knew anything at all. The messenger didn't even care as he told Lamere the news of his wife's death. Saying that the sky looked a little cloudy would have been the same to this guy.

C'mon, why would a level 2 Knower be at their door for such a message? The Controller just said, "Your sinful wife has defied the laws of the holy Exalter. Her work detail is cancelled, her rations are terminated, and she is in our custody. Forget her or live in misery."

There was no more explanation, there was no mercy, and there was no sympathy. The Knowers could have easily sent a letter to their mailbox, like many other Derogate families had experienced during such a tragedy. But no, a level 2 division Knower came to the door. They were the worst division that the Exalter established. They did all the dirty work, all the killing, all the beating, and all the radical orders sent out by the Exalter. It was whispered by some Derogates that these level 2 Knowers had even taken people at random and publicly asked them to accept the Exalter or deny him with the feared ultimatum.

Acceptance granted you a pardon, but not the right to become a Knower: just another day to breathe. Denial resulted in a public beheading right there and then, which no one verified officially. Level 2 Knowers were part of an elite military operation. What was the need for those black eye coverings they always wore? Why weren't the Derogates allowed to see their eyes?

They carried weapons and had devices that fit in their ear that enabled them to talk to each other, even without words sometimes. They had attached body armor as if they needed it and always traveled in the same utility vehicles, equipped with many advanced electronics. Hah, what was electricity to the Derogates? The only electricity they got in their black suet villages would be an unfortunate lightning storm. The level 2 Knowers were also referred to as Controllers. They were absolutely everything that the word *intimidating* would define. It was said that after training was completed by a level 2 Knower, the Exalter himself would give each man or woman a new name. Their old name was never uttered again, as the Exalter said they were a new creation now.

The Controller walked back into his utility vehicle that day. In his dark glasses, a visual display appeared on the left lens as an audio signal also went into his earpiece. The Controller knew what it meant and waited for the retinal scan. Light-blue lines went side to side on his lenses vertically side to side. This was no regular retinal scan. The scan went beyond the eye to make sure the blood behind the eye was not only circulating, but also an acceptable alive human temperature. This method was put into place to ensure that the recipient was not only the right person but also that he was alive to prevent messages getting to those disgraceful Derogates or anyone else willing to defy the holy Exalter.

Beep ...

The scan was complete. The controller's message was coming in. The Exalter's voice was every command, even though it wasn't him speaking in real time. It was a device that copied his voice and gave orders. This time, it alerted, "Report to the black suet village number eighteen for extraction of Derogates suspected to be illegally practicing the detestable worship of the false god. All deifiers are to be executed at the platform of their village."

Like a drone, the soldier replied, "Consider it done, my lord." He went on to his next order without giving a thought to the news he had just given. The Derogates were nothing to him, and they deserved nothing. They should have had less than what they were given.

Chapter 5

Janae walked early in the dark morning with Tyrisha, just like every day, Thursday through Tuesday. Janae was medium height, with a slim figure. Her distinct oval face and blondish-brown hair set off her rarely seen smile. She always wore an expression that communicated she had a chip on her shoulder. She was upset about something—or maybe many things. Tyrisha, on the other hand, had a much happier disposition. Her naturally tan skin was desired by everyone. Her wavy dark brown hair stretched to her shoulders. Like Janae, Tyrisha had an oval little face, with a distinct, small chin. She stood shorter than Janae, and her figure was larger than Janae's. Both of the young girls were a single man's hope to encounter.

You would think they would be tired from the hard work. The difference was that they were both so used to the routine that it just seemed normal; the long days never seemed to drag. The walk to the Derogate facilities was the perk of the day for many of the Derogates.

"Someday, all this is going to be over," Tyrisha said as she glared up at the dark blue sky.

Janae's lips pressed together as she shook her head and replied, "You know, I don't believe in all that mumbo-jumbo, Tyrisha." The girls had been in the same village since birth, and at age six, they had both begun the walk to their duty every day, finding comfort in the similarities. Now, the differences seemed more present than ever.

"Janae, I wonder why in the world you keep staying here if you don't even believe in the Only. I don't want you to leave, but really, why are you here?"

Janae talked as she looked down at the dull ground: "It's really simple, Tyrisha. I stay for my mother, my father, and my little sister, Tayara."

It wasn't as simple as Janae put it. She had spent countless days thinking about the garbage lifestyle she lived. She was hated by the Derogates, and she didn't like it. She was a servant and had no idea of luxury, but to serve those who had it was sickening. She felt every temptation to have an easy life like the Knowers. After all, what kind of loving creator would allow such suffering for her? Wasn't she loved more than that? She knew that if she became a Derogate, so much would change. Sure, there were ideas she didn't like, such as being taken as a multiple wife by some man and then the body sharing, which made her nervous every time she thought about it, but also dangerously tempting. She wasn't even sure that she believed in anything. The one thing she did know was that even faking it to be a Knower would be worth it.

When Tyrisha didn't respond, Janae said, "Tyrisha? What makes you so sure that the Only even exists? I mean, look at what we are going through. Look at what we are doing. Just look at how we are treated. Shouldn't it be the other way around, if we are the Only's people?"

Tyrisha smiled without showing teeth, nodded once, and then calmly answered, "I know the Only is real because I can feel him. He has shown me subtle things in my life that could be mistaken for coincidence instead of miracles. The way it just went, instead of blessings. These things are as little as protection from punishment from Knowers and protection against their abuse. The larger things are providing clothes, shelter, and food for me and my family. He has healed me from sicknesses, and in this time of trouble, I know what comes next, and that feeling is peaceful."

Janae warned, "You had better be careful with that book no one knows you have. You realize that's brainwashing stuff you got your hands on, right, girly? If you keep reading those stories and talking about us being saved from this mess, you are going to be seriously disappointed."

With that, Tyrisha could tell that Janae had hit her limit for religious talk for the day. Janae veered away from Tyrisha and headed for her cleansing at the Derogate facility before she began her day of work. All Janae could think about was how all that Only talk was a load of trash.

She thought to herself, *Yeah, right, he is gonna save us. Oh, I had better look up. Here I have to serve people and clean up their garbage, and for what? They breathe the same air I do, yet I am an insect to them. Some god, some life, some dumb idea ... Psssht.*

Chapter 6

Lamere and Leviticus never talked about June's disappearance. How could they, when it was too hard? Being a Derogate meant you had to be tough, and you had to learn it quickly. They hugged and comforted each other but never mourned together. It was no secret they both had held their times of isolated weeping. It was an awful day when June disappeared. That was also the day that Leviticus was so angry he chose to forget the Only. He just didn't want anything to do with him anymore. Why would the Only do this? Why would he especially do this to his mother, who was so right and pure? She followed his ways and knew his ways. It didn't make sense to him. He was so angry, and he even looked up at the skies in the pathetic excuse for a forest surrounding his village and cursed the Only. He was so mad at the Only.

In the same sense, he wanted to believe that the Only didn't even exist, so how could he be angry at something that didn't exist? Lamere knew that Leviticus was angry and numb to the teachings of the Only after that tragedy. However, he didn't stop praising the Only and looking forward to the day when he would be reunited with his precious soulmate, June. He knew that the Only was all good, and some good would happen out of this; it had to be either the Only's will or an attempt by the evil one. They would be together again, with no threat of being separated again. They would be safe together … forever.

"Father, I don't hear you in there. Are you okay?"

Leviticus had just told his father that there was rumor of this new proclaimed Exalter coming into power on a one-world-order-type of government level. Lamere went into the eating room to get them some water. Then they could talk some politics and think about future oppression and what it meant for them.

Leviticus got up and walked into the eating room of his father's house, but no one was there. He looked left, right, and then all around. What was that on the ground? His father's clothes were just sitting there on the floor, stacked like a pile of pancakes. He rushed over to the pile; underneath the clothes were his father's shoes.

Leviticus realized the truth of his entire oppressed existence. Well, whatever, he wasn't going to be convinced that easily. He searched the whole house and even looked outside the door of his father's house. It had been raining, and all the footprints were washed away; there no fresh prints to show if his father had walked out the door. He came back to the pile of clothes, sat on a chair, and then closed his eyes, thinking, as the memory of his mother entered.

"Someday, Leviticus, when the false one comes," she said, "the great Only will take all his believers into heaven, away from the evil. Then the trials will begin as the 2,555 days of punishment take place. Meanwhile, the false god rules the lands everywhere. Those who don't believe in the Only will be given the chance to believe, and he will take them in as his own. All the others will serve the false god."

Leviticus closed his eyes as a tear dropped onto his cheek. The memory of his mother mixed with this intense experience brought him to a place of overbearing emotion. He began to speak the words he had chosen to discredit for the majority of his life: "The Only must be *real*."

Chapter 7

Finally, it was one o'clock, and Nicolai wasn't eager to go back to his household, even though his work shift was over. The day was dark, even a little after noon, and the skies held a constant gloom. The rain had poured all day long, with a constant flow and no sign of letting up. Nicolai exited his office, scanned out with his right hand, and headed to the elevator with a slow pace, while everyone else around him seemed to be power walking. He even missed the elevator and waited for the next one to come up.

Tink.

The elevator door opened, and he entered alone. He thought how funny it was that years back, there would have been security cameras in the elevator and security staff to watch them, but they were now powered off. After the Exalter finally revealed his presence, he seemed to know everything. Somehow, he saw everything, and somehow, he made it peaceful. The promise of the peace treaty had continued for the past seven years, holding out hope for everyone. He was everywhere, all at once, as if he had clone of himself watching in every area; they seemed to report back to him constantly.

So why was it that Nicolai didn't feel so peaceful? His thoughts that day were just like the weather: dreary. Nicolai tried to pretend like he was happy doing his computer work, content with the issues at home, as if he felt whole. He knew he wasn't like the others, but too many changes were taking place. He felt like he was watching a map being drawn around him, and he had no idea where the roads were or which ones to even take. The demographics of his life were sketchy from the beginning, when it started.

Tink.

Again, the elevator opened, and Nicolai viewed the already-empty parking lot. His Knower vehicle knew when he was near, as the motion sensor by the car handle initiated the sensor waiting to detect the device in his right hand. A *beep* was followed by the single sound of four locks opening simultaneously. The drive home wasn't even far enough to make him feel like he had gone anywhere. Twenty minutes seemed like a short breath as this man seemed to think about so many things. What was the initiative in all the work he did? Why did Nicolai feel so unaccomplished? He thought to himself, *Why is it that the Exalter is on earth with humans? I mean, mere mortals? Why doesn't he just take us all to heaven or whatever?*

A question like that could have earned him a severed spinal cord, as it sounded very close to blasphemy. The dreaded guillotines were always ready for a new victim. Everyone knew that blasphemy against the Exalter earned you a ticket to what they jokingly called a quick and speedy trial. The joke was in that there was no trial, no jury, and no waiting for judgment in a cell. Instead, you were executed within the hour, once approval was rendered. Cells and jails were pretty much obsolete anymore. Ever since the Exalter gave what the Seer called the great pardon, all prisoners and inmates had been released in the United States and then globally. The Exalter had forgiven them for their sins and trespasses. He had told them how he loved them and how they deserved mercy. First, the ex-prisoners were divided into Knowers or Derogates. Second, they were placed into a Knower division or Derogate black suet village. Many of the prisoners were taken into the Knower military squads. Finally, the ex-prisoners welcomed or hated their new life.

Nicolai took the right-hand turn onto Rest Avenue and turned into his driveway. He lived in a standard marriage settlement where a man and a woman were married. The modern neighborhoods housed married women to women or men to men depending on the set up. There were even neighborhoods for mixed gender couples. The modern and mixed neighborhoods were multiplying much faster than the standard ones.

He entered his house after sensors detected his presence and unlocked the door. As he entered, there was one of his three body partners, Kiyana. Kiyana was Nicolai's favorite wife of them all. After all, she was his first before the Exalter changed every aspect of their lives. Deep down, he didn't even want to have three wives. It was all the same mandates set out by the Exalter. Everyone was being taught to indulge in each other sexually, to do what feels good, and to live life to the fullest amount of pleasure possible. For Nicolai, the most pleasurable idea would be to go back in time and take who Kiyana was three years ago and teleport onto a quiet tropical island. Just her and just him, with no one else—absolutely no one.

Chapter 8

Kiyana was coming down from a drinking binge, like usual. Even in her post-drunken state, she was beautiful to Nicolai. Many women color their hair blonde, but Kiyana's was natural. Her blonde hair was the perfect texture and so manageable. He loved gazing into her blue eyes. She was just as tall as Nicolai was and no stranger to being athletic. Nicolai loved that cute side smile she wore when she was happy. She saw Nicolai enter the house as his wet coverings dripped, and he shook off the water as goose bumps formed on each arm.

"Nicolai, I am so glad you're home," she said, slurring in her speech. "I was getting lonely."

Nicolai paused and clenched his jaw, and then remembering who she used to be, he stepped forward to embrace her. He hugged her tightly, as if to say more than a greeting, and his nostrils filled with a different scent than that of Kiyana's usual perfume.

He broke the grasp of the hug and said, "Kiyana, whose cologne is that?"

She answered with no shame, "Honey, it's just something new Cedro is trying."

Nicolai's mood was shattered in an instant and he asked, "He's been here again?"

Cedro was a first-class division Knower, just like Kiyana, the kind of Knower who made Nicolai's blood boil. All these first-class Knowers did was eat, drink, body share, and experiment in ways to get high off of whatever they could find, sell, or barter. Some had obsessions of exercise to be the most attractive, and others just wanted to abuse drugs. Some had both views. What did they have for responsibility? What did they know at all, if anything? More than likely, they didn't spend five minutes sober in any day. The whole idea of multiple body sharing disgusted Nicolai, and his attempts to hide it were less than convincing.

"Kiyana, do you really think this is okay?" he snapped.

Kiyana grew annoyed and said, "Nicolai, c'mon, you know my allegiance is to you. I love you."

Nicolai's eyes pierced into Kiyana's. His angry face and clenched jaw were further annoying Kiyana, as she took offense.

"Who are *you* to question the will of the almighty Exalter?" she asked. "He has made it clean and pure for all of us to body share with whomever we want, when we want. He encourages it, and to speak against it is blasphemy."

There was the word that every Knower threatened people with. It seemed to be the only thing to threaten peace anymore was blasphemy.

Nicolai fired back, "Kiyana, the Exalter may have said it is right to do, but you know it doesn't feel right to me. I just want to have you and for you to have me. I want to feel like what we have is special and unique, to the point where the only person you want to body share with is me."

Kiyana looked puzzled, as her facial contortion communicated to Nicolai that she was saying, "What?"

"Oh, forget it. I'm going for a drive to cool off."

Nicolai had taken off his jacket already and just walked outside in the rain to his car. It's as if he wanted to cool his hot feelings of anger and jealousy off in the cold rain. The depressing cold outdoors felt somehow aligned to the feelings he had inside.

As Nicolai walked down the driveway, Kiyana opened the door and called out, "Nicolai, don't go. We can go upstairs right now if you want to."

Nicolai felt like he was vomiting emotionally. The only reply Kiyana got was a car door that slammed shut.

Once in his car, he snapped, "Ugh, are you kidding me? You don't get a thing."

He went for a long drive and decided to take some roads he never had before. These roads were the streets where you would always see the Derogates taking their walks to their black suet villages or to the sanitation facilities.

Chapter 9

"Tyrisha, where are you going?"

Tyrisha knew better than to answer. It wasn't legal for a Derogate to address a Knower. She kept her mouth shut, turned around to face the headmaster, Mr. Tirian, and then pretended she had something to stare at on the floor as she lowered her face downward.

"My wives and I just finished having a meal in the resting room, and we have made quite a mess. I wouldn't find it acceptable to have all that uneaten food, dishes, and bottles lying around overnight. The floor no doubt needs a thorough cleaning in there before you go, as well. Well, quit standing there as if you're a dead statue; get it done."

She brought her head up slightly and then lowered her head again in submission to the headmaster she had been assigned to. Tirian and his three wives tried to walk up the staircase, as they all were laughing and kissing each other. One of the Tirian's wives laughed and made sure Tyrisha heard her say, "Like she has anything more important to do or anywhere to go."

Thank the Only that the house was large enough that when the bed chambers door shut, the noise they created was also extinguished. Tyrisha cleaned up the mess those savage pigs had made and then got a bucket; mopping the floor would make the Knowers there feel pampered. She didn't judge them or think too harshly against them. Instead, she felt compassion for them and thought about how badly they needed the Only. All those Knowers could do was fill their life with junk so they wouldn't have to really think. They never had meaningful thoughts, and they were slaves to their addictions. They thought their lives were so full, yet Tyrisha spent too much time at that house and saw how empty their lives really were. In fact, their lives were so empty that they had to keep their wine glasses filled, to at least have a false sense of fullness.

Tyrisha began her cold walk home. Every black suet village was on the north side of town, as if the Exalter was letting them all know he would like them to be a bit colder than everyone else.

She stepped outside and draped a large piece of cloth around the homemade umbrella constructed of sticks and thin rope, that would support the cloth and keep at least some of this rain off of her. She took one deep breath in as if to say silently, "Okay, here we go," and she headed home.

The sun had gone down, and all the other Knowers had already gone home, so she was rather alone. It didn't seem to bother her. She prayed to the Only on her walk. She was praying silently in her head. To be caught praying to the Only was grounds for beheading, and it felt exciting to talk with the Only in her head and convey her thoughts, her prayers, and her hopes for a better life.

A Knower vehicle came up behind her at a slow pace. What was a Knower vehicle doing on these roads? she wondered. This wasn't a Controller vehicle, so something was really out of place. Tyrisha grew nervous as the vehicle stopped beside her. The window rolled down, and a handsome man in the darkness of the car said, "It is cold out here, and to make things worse, the rain is cold. Why don't you get in, and I will drive you to your home?"

Tyrisha couldn't believe that first, this stranger had addressed her kindly and even wanted to drive her home. It was forbidden to have such contact with a Knower, as ordered by the Seer straight from the Exalter himself.

Tyrisha responded predictably: "Do you not know that it is forbidden for us to be together?"

Nicolai's anger at Kiyana was calmed by this girl's presence. He shot back, "Then why did you just address me, which is also forbidden?"

Tyrisha smiled gently.

"Please, I am not going to harm you," he added, "and to be honest, today is not a fantastic day for me. It seems the end of your day was like the middle of mine. Doing something nice would make me feel better… please."

Tyrisha looked all around and then reluctantly walked to the other side of the Knower's vehicle. She stood there as she didn't know how to enter the car. Nicolai reached over and opened the door for her. The first thing she noticed was the curve that went into her lower back. It seemed to feel supportive and not like all the straight-backed chairs at her village home. It felt nice, but she kept her wits about her and was careful not to desire such luxuries. The car began to drive on, as Nicolai headed for black suet village three. He could tell where to go because of the number 113 on Tyrisha's shoes and clothes. After all, Nicolai was familiar with all the numbering, all the technical stuff, and all the Knower systems from his position. Most of the Knowers could hardly work three hours, and yet Nicolai wouldn't mind six hours a day and was often reprimanded for going over three hours.

"My given name is Nicolai," he said. "What is yours?"

Still being cautious, she kept her most serious tone. "My name is Tyrisha. I don't understand why you are helping me."

Nicolai smiled and said, "You have a really nice name. So Tyrisha, tell me, do you believe in true love? That is, more specifically, what does true love mean to the Derogate belief system?"

Nicolai was asking about information that Tyrisha knew even speaking about could get her killed. However, this Nicolai had already broken the law of no communication. And Tyrisha knew a day might come when she would have to take a stand. She was ready. She was ready to die for the Only if she had to, so it was time to be full of courage.

She replied slowly, "True love is when the Only creates one woman and one man to be together in all ways, with purity. It is when that man and woman can think only of how to better love each other and be a benefit to each other's life. They want to better know each other, share who they really are with each other, unfold their deepest thoughts, unravel their secret hopes, unwind their deepest desires, and reveal their hidden secrets with trust. Most of all, they want to better each other by loving one another the way the Only loves us. As a public demonstration, they have the covenant promise ceremony held in secret, where they commit to one another in faithful love, acceptance, and submission."

Nicolai was just caught in this girl's words. She was too busy thinking of the powerful description she would hope to have someday. It took Nicolai a minute before he answered, "Wow, it sounds like you have really given this love business some great thought. You said two things that stuck out to me, Tyrisha. You said that it would be one woman and one man created for only one another, is that right? You also said somewhere in there about faithful love. Does that mean they are faithful in a way where in your Derogate belief, they only love and body share with each other? No other sharing, emotionally or physically, is that right?"

"Yes, Nicolai, that is exactly right." Tyrisha had never even addressed a Knower directly.

Nicolai stopped the vehicle at the black gate, signifying the pathetic main entrance to black suet village three. He reached across and unlocked her door with his right hand. He could have done it manually, but he wanted to be nearer to this woman who, in his mind, he would give up the world to have. His love for Kiyana was almost gone, and he was holding on to the edge. He also pulled the handle, as he knew Tyrisha probably didn't know how to get out of a car.

"Tyrisha, it was so nice to meet you. Thank you for explaining to me something I wish I had. Now don't tell anyone about this, and if anyone asks, tell them you gained favor at your headmaster's household and were given a ride because of the bad weather by a landscaper."

Tyrisha had never felt so honored in all of her years. She had been mistreated, spat at, and hated, but now, a Knower had been nice to her. She thought that all the Knowers were the same brainwashed replicas of each other. This man seemed to erase years of undeserved treatment in minutes. Who was he? He didn't seem to belong, or maybe he wasn't a headmaster yet, with his assigned three wives to take his mind off of love. Was he an angel? It didn't matter; he had been nice to her when she had been given nothing but abuse.

As Tyrisha departed, she said, "Thank you, Nicolai, for the ride home. You have been so kind, and I hope you get what you are hoping for."

She began the muddy walk to her village home. Nicolai sat in the car as he watched her walk to her assigned house. The mud was over taking her worn shoes on her way.

He found himself wishing that Kiyana was more like Tyrisha. Who was he kidding? He would have left Kiyana for this Tyrisha, right then and right there. She was peaceful, honest, and true, and he knew she would be faithful. That word "*faithful*" was something from the stone age and had long since been extinct. Something was so different about this girl, like a breath of fresh air.

Nicolai again spoke to himself aloud: "Who am I kidding? No one like her would ever accept me. If I left the Knowers, they would certainly kill me to make an example. Ahhh, what are you thinking, Nick?"

After all, there was no record of any Knower ever becoming a Derogate. It's not hard to predict what the end result would be to that one.

Chapter 10

Leviticus rushed home quickly from black suet village number seven, where his father lived. Leviticus hated the word "Derogate," but everywhere he looked, there was the definition of Derogate panic. Derogates were crying, rushing out of villages yelling, and crowds were forming. Leviticus decided it was best to take the forest paths back to village three, in order to see to the safety of his beloved daughter, Tyrisha, and his wife, Zeneth. As he traveled slowly through the back woods, Leviticus could hear many voices in the trees. What were these Derogates doing in the woods? He knew that Derogates went into the forest to catch whatever they could to eat, but such a meeting was never heard of, and leaving the village was punishable if caught.

The man on the top of the hill placed his right foot on a log as he held a walking stick.

"Now you have seen it all with your own eyes," he told the crowd. "The Knowers have stripped us of our freedom, our rights, and now, many of our family members are gone with their black magic tricks. I tell you that I did not believe in the Only until now. Now, well now, I don't know about the so-called Only, but I know the Exalter is evil. I am willing to go out on a branch and say the stories the true believers taught of the Only might be true. They have vanished into thin air, just as promised by those who told the stories of the Only. So what does this mean for us?"

Numerous people in the crowd began shouting; one said, "They took my family!"

Another man cried out, "We need revenge for this. I've had it!"

And one woman said loudly, "I have nothing to lose anymore. It means we are going to have to choose a side. Live or die. They will want to identify us all somehow with markings, numbers, or those incisions. They will give us the choice to worship the Exalter and his legion or face death. Should we fight? The answer is yes. However, we are incredibly outnumbered. We are incredibly outgunned. We are also incredibly without life-sustaining supplies. They have made us dependent on them. So the time is now. Gather your things, gather any supplies, and gather what loved ones you have left. We must retreat deep into the country and gather an alliance. I will not bow down to this corruption. Who is with me?"

The broken men and women in the crowd felt strengthened despite their great losses. There were even teenagers in the crowd who had not disappeared. It seemed the very young children were all gone, distinguished from the older ones. After all, family was the only thing from keeping them from rioting. The tattered and worn clothing of all the men and women looked like they were already in the middle of a war. They had numbered clothes and shoes, poor hygiene, and an abundance of nothing. There was indeed not much left to lose.

"I said, 'Who is with me?'" she repeated.

The small crowd of maybe thirty all yelled shouts of "Yeah!" and "We are!" They all gathered their things, and some left to gather their belongings from their mud homes.

Leviticus could hardly believe what was transpiring right in front of his eyes. First, his mother was taken from him, and then his father. Now there was a possibility that his daughter and wife were also gone. He worried about their well-being more than ever. What if they had been taken? What was he going to do then? What if they weren't taken? The confusion and movements going on would be dangerous. He knew chaos would start to shape, and those two beautiful young women in danger was something he did not want to think about. His came closer to his anxiety-filled destination. Finally, he was at the north side of the northerly located village. The sun was showing a small tip as he looked right toward the westward skyline.

People were frantic in his village, and he could see Knower vehicle headlights in the distance, coming from the south. He sprinted toward his house. The run made his heart pound in anticipation. The closer he got, the harder his heart pounded: 109, 110, 111, 112, and then finally, house 113. Before he opened the door, he knew Tyrisha was home. After all, this was Wednesday, the day of worship for the Knowers. During those days, all the Knowers would gather in temples constructed by the Exalter and give him praise for the prosperity, praise for the peace, and praise for his kindness. Leviticus's anger from such thoughts quickly faded as he opened the door to his mud hut. Even that thought made his eyes start to water, as he thought how he used to make humor out of it to amuse his wife, Zeneth. They needed humor in such terrible oppression, like a diabetic needs insulin. The house seemed empty, but maybe, just maybe, Tyrisha had been smart enough to hide somewhere, knowing her father would return for her.

He called out, "Zeneth? Tyrisha? Girls, are you home? Please be here."

He walked into the eating area, where remnants of a recent cooked meal filled the air. The wood had smoldered out, and there was his answer: Zeneth's clothes sat in a pile with the shoes on the bottom, just as he found his father's. He sighed in relief that at least no one else had her but also felt the extreme loneliness without her there. Even when Leviticus was out working the streets for the Knowers, he felt better knowing Zeneth would be there at home, waiting for him that night.

Now, life seemed to have a new meaning. That meaning felt like no meaning at all. He could feel her absence, like a piece of him was amputated and taken away across the cosmos. Leviticus began the slow, defeated walk into Tyrisha's room, fearing he was now completely alone. On her cot, there was exactly what he expected to find. After all, both his wife and daughter were devoted believers and shared their faith, prayers, and hope in bonding love. Tyrisha's clothes and nighttime socks were laid out on the bed. She would usually be resting or reading there. He put his head down, and the tears that he held in finally released. His sobs filled the empty house and were released like a dam breaking. He sat on her bed and wailed as he touched her shirt and tried to take in the memory of her smell. He held the shirt close to his chest, hugging it. He had Zeneth's shirt in his left hand and brought the shirts together on his chest. He pretended he was really hugging the both of them with all the love his body could give, as he embraced the shirts tightly.

To the right of the bed was ... what was that? His grip on the shirts loosened, and his right hand touched the tattered old book that Tyrisha must have been reading. A homemade paper cover showed the title: *How to Know the Exalter.* He looked surprised as he opened the cover. The paper was thin, worn, and faded. He starting reading the book and realized exactly what it was. It was the book that many said each village had. It was clever to disguise the book with such a title so it would not be investigated. He had never seen the book and had only heard stories of it. Why would Tyrisha hide this from him? Well, before this morning, he knew exactly why she hid it from him. She knew he had been quiet about the Only, and the disappearance of his mother absolutely rocked his faith to the point of disbelief and hatred.

The discovery of the holy book changed Leviticus's sorrow to a realization that he now had a purpose. But wait a minute ... now, he had possession of a ticket to the decapitating machine. He had to get out of there. He stared out the window, deep in thought, and decided it had to be now. He had to get this book to others so that they could be saved before the well-known story of the 2,555 days of punishment destroyed them all.

Chapter 11

The global network kicked on in the Exalter's temple located in Nicolai's neighborhood. It was, of course, Wednesday, the day of worship and celebration of wining and dining for the Knowers. The Exalter wasn't wearing his golden, gem-filled crown. He only wore it when he was in a global meeting or making an important appearance. After all, the Exalter was the solo media craze. There was no more coverage of movie stars; there were no more celebrities. It was a miracle that those annoying shows were finally gone, anyway. Rather than that people worship, the only worship was to be aimed at the Exalter. Any type of news coverage spotlighting a person was absolutely forbidden. The only person to be showed in a view like that was the Exalter. Networks had to be very careful of what they showed about other people, so as to not take the glory from the Exalter in any way.

"You all have seen my powerful judgment now. I knew this time would come, and I have been trying to wait and give mercy to the unbelieving Derogates, waiting for them to come to me. My mercy has been great, but the time has come where the false believers will not change. By my words, I have destroyed all the true believers in the false god. They are now condemned to suffer in the fire for eternity."

The Exalter looked confident like that of a strong lion surrounded by starved and weakened animals. No one would dare challenge him.

He continued on, "My children, I know your thoughts, and I tell you, do not worry. I have known my plans for you, and they are pleasurable. I knew the great judgment would come, and I have been constructing replacements for the Derogates for months."

A wall rose to the left shoulder of the Exalter, revealing a machine shaped like a man. It was made of a polished, shiny metal and had blasting eyes that shone a sparkly blue.

"What you see behind me is your guardian. These guardians are linked to your specific implant and will serve you in your household. Over the next three months, all over the world, we will all work together to get every Knower their own guardian. They are here to protect you. And from what, you might ask. I tell you, there are some Derogates left who believe they can retreat deep into hiding and revolt against me and the service they owe to you. I will make sure each of my Knower children has their own special protector guardian.

"Henceforth, I am also establishing the incision for all leftover Derogates, as they will be taken to labor for us as they have always done. They will build us great cities, new fruitful economies, worshiping temples, roadways, and any work deemed necessary by the global sovereignty."

The Knowers across the world listened to the Exalter give this great news. It interested everyone, and they had their eyes glued to the screen. The temples were silent, as usual. Outbursts or talking during the speaking of the Exalter would earn a consequence of a week of solitary confinement.

"Any Derogate that refuses this incision is an enemy of both you and I. We will imprison those who refuse the mark and rid the earth of those who move against me. However, my mercy is great, and I will give them all a second chance to serve me by allowing such an offense to be forgiven following forced labor in prison, to teach their body a lesson of hard work for nothing gained without me. For my obedient children, I have commanded that each and every Knower be assigned a personal guardian to go with them everywhere they travel, in order to protect and help them. The guardians are a magnificent creation for all of you, as my gift to the children I love. They will help you if you are injured in an accident and offer other benefits to your life. Enjoy my gift to you, the peace I bring you, and to the future of our prosperity and enjoyment of life. Remember, my judgment has been merciful, and I have given you all many gifts to be thankful for, and that is why I know you love me and worship me as your Exalted Only."

The screen disappeared as the crowd said in unison, "Holy Exalter, master of the universe, let your will be done great and sovereign lord."

Nicolai looked around at all these drunk and drugged-out idiots surrounding him, bowing like programmed circus monkeys. This news was stupid, but Nicolai wasn't surprised. Wait a minute, what was this? What did he see now in front of his own eyes? It would have been half-tolerable to hide the truth without seeing it. Kiyana, his first wife, was all over that over that lazy, no-good pretty boy gym rat. Nicolai saw only the two of them and gazed with thoughts of wistful murder in mind.

That is, only for Cedro, of course. He watched as they snuck out of the temple. Nicolai followed, undetected, and knew they were going back to Cedro's household. He took a different route in order to avoid being discovered, but his perfect timing left him watching them pull up in Cedro's car. What a sick feeling it was for Nicolai to know his wife was with another man, and he was watching it all unfold. He could see the silhouette of Kiyana's head from the driver's side door. Cedro pulled into his garage, as they were being very sneaky. Nicolai was now in a side alley, waiting. For what, even he didn't know. He sat in his car for forty minutes, thinking about what he would do. The same amount of time, he was disgusted by thinking about what he knew they were doing inside. His heart filled with rage, his angry blood surged, and his core temperature rose as he felt his face flush. He knew that if he was making a move, it needed to be today. The new guardians would be in place, and of course, it would protect Nicolai, and he would never be able to slip away from his own guardian. Worse yet, a guardian would be protecting Cedro. The guardian would no doubt feel like an overbearing, inquisitive mother. He knew he was GPS-chipped, like the others, but they didn't even know it, and they didn't even understand the capacity the chip had if the Exalter ordered it.

He shut his car door slowly. He decided it would be best to sneak in and wait for Kiyana to leave. She would have to sneak home quickly to lie about how she was mingling after worship and some other bag of garbage. He went to the basement, and sure enough, he already knew the schematics of that property. He had used his job to access the security codes and also each floor layout. He used a code in the basement window from Knower utility workers that were used in cases of warming and cooling systems if a Knower wasn't home. It was deemed offensive to enter a home when the person wasn't home, but accessing the basement was easy. The door to each level had a passcode. Nicolai's wallet contained each individual passcode for every section of the house, as there was no way he could memorize it. He didn't even have to look around because all the brainwashed zombies were still at worship as he casually walked up to that basement window on the opposite side of Cedro's bedroom.

He entered the passcode, and the window at ground level popped open. Nicolai slid in with some contortion. He shut the window, rearmed it, and then began his way to the next level.

"Huh? Ohhh," he whispered as his left foot got caught on a cord, and he fell against the wall. His fall had seemed to separate a piece of the wall. Nicolai had spent hours looking at Cedro's house plans, fantasizing about what he would do and how he would do it. Never was anything but an empty hall in the area where he bumped into some type of thin wall sticking out. His curiosity seemed to overpower the idea of murdering the man who had seduced his wife. He looked around for something and found a piece of metal to pry the piece off. First, it appeared as though the piece of wall would pop off, and then it simply slid on invisible tracks. The white door slid to the right and uncovered a soundproof, insulated room. Nicolai's flashlight pointed above the strange room, and he discovered that new piping was running above it. It was easy to tell, as the new piping was not faded like the other pipes.

As Nicolai slid the doors farther, his flashlight illuminated a door with black bars. He thought to himself, *This sicko has a hidden prison cell? For what? What is he doing down here, and who is he doing it to?* The door slid open and revealed a little room with a dim light, which fell upon a small sleeping pad and a dirty cup and bowl on the floor. There was a toilet in the corner of the little room. What was in the other corner?

Nicolai looked closely and viewed clothes in the corner and then shoes side by side, facing away from the wall. He thought to himself that a body could have been sitting there with their back against the wall. He looked for the number and saw it, after some focusing in the darkness. It was household 252. Nicolai took the mental picture in, remembering number 252. What importance did that have in any of this?

Nicolai shut the sliding door that hid the cell and headed up the stairs of the basement. He entered the passcode, opened the door, rearmed the door, and then began his careful ascent to the top of the house, where he would get his vengeance on Cedro.

Nicolai heard a man's voice. "Kiyana, tell Nicolai I said hello."

"I can't believe how smug you are, Cedro. I have to get out of here quick so that he doesn't notice me gone."

Cedro complained, "All right, but I will miss you until next time."

Nicolai was at the end of a hall now on the main floor as he clenched his jaw listening to Kiyana and Cedro walk down the stairs, playing their little secret game of filth. After Kiyana exited the door, Nicolai waited for the right chance. Cedro shut the door and walked to his kitchen to make something to eat. He could hear him promoting himself as he said, "Oh yeah, I got it good."

Nicolai decided it was the right time. He crept up behind Cedro with his flashlight in his right hand. He stayed low as he crept behind him. By the time Cedro heard something, it was too late. A thud came from the impact of the flashlight to the back of Cedro's head as Nicolai completed the swing. He took off his backpack, which had been in his trunk. He had fantasized so often of killing Cedro that he had supplies ready for the right time, even though he never thought he'd really do it.

Now here he was, and the feelings of hatred were now somewhat mixed with nervousness. If Kiyana would do this with one person, what would stop her from doing it again, even if Cedro was gone? He used the rope to tie Cedro's hands behind his back and carried him down the stairs, sitting him in a chair in the basement. He tied his ankles to the legs of the chair and even tied a rope around his chest and around the back of the chair.

He slapped Cedro and said calmly, "Wake up; wake up, you scum."

Cedro regained consciousness but appeared very confused. Maybe it was from the booze or from the blow to the head.

Cedro looked like a good old boy. That is, except for a little lion tattoo on his neck. His tanning bed leathery skin and luxurious kept black hair is what usually got him noticed. His fine facial hair allowed him to stay handsomely clean shaven. The man was dedicated to beauty, that is of himself. He had ridiculously white teeth, waxed eyebrows, and an obsession with exercising. Just under six foot, he wasn't a body builder, but he could definitely hold his own.

Cedro spoke as he tried to focus his eyes, "Nicolai? Is that you?"

He tried to move and realized he was bound, as the rope didn't give. His breath escaped him as he had used it to make an all-out effort to flex his muscles and escape the ropes. He waited a second and mustered up a sentence: "What? Are you here to kill me because of Kiyana? C'mon, we're not doing anything illegal. If you kill me, don't you think the Exalter will find out? You better let me go before this goes any further and you regret it."

Nicolai was in control now and sounded like it, as he said to the captive man, "Oh, Cedro, we have so much to talk about. I certainly am here because of my disapproval of you and Kiyana. But we already know that, don't we? However, something else has come to my attention."

Nicolai turned Cedro and the chair to the right, where he was facing the hidden room. He walked over to the panel and opened it up, shined his flashlight inside, and said, "First, why don't you tell me what this is all about?"

Chapter 12

This house is always in pretty good shape because I don't ever skip corners, June thought to herself. She was referring to Cedro's house, of course. It was hard to gather strength to do much cleaning at her own home each night, after all the cooking and what-not. She was proud of her work, proud of her husband, Lamere, and especially proud of the family her son, Leviticus, had put together (with the assistance of the Only, naturally). In the background of her cleaning lay a danger. If you could read the thoughts of Cedro's wife, Xyla, you would think you were watching a nature channel, as a black panther hides in the shadows, waiting to attack its unsuspecting prey.

June had to be careful about her work. She knew that Xyla did not like her. It was obvious in the way she talked to June and looked at her. The best thing for June to do was just to avoid Xyla at all costs. Whatever kind of work she could find, she would stay out of her way. Dusting with a Q-tip sounded better than feeling the tension around that mean woman.

Xyla couldn't talk to anyone about it. She was just so explosively jealous of June that it consumed her thoughts. She had caught Cedro flirting with her many times. She would never flirt back or even talk; she just did her work as usual, but Xyla wasn't blind; she knew that June was uniquely beautiful, gifted with kindness, worked hard, and was good at everything, as far as she could see. What if Cedro added her as his fourth wife and body partner? He would be commended in the community for converting a Derogate into a Knower. His egocentrism would be doubled by two. He would invent a new self, with her by his side.

He would love her more than me, she thought. There was no doubt she would be put on the back burner, and she wasn't going to let that happen, no matter what.

Xyla had already formulated her plan, but she needed the timing to be right.

The day finally came. The music tone went off in the house as someone was at the door. Xyla looked down from her third-floor master bedroom. Her eyes focused as it was what she was waiting for. A Knower utility worker was at the door, doing a routine service check. Xyla hurried down the stairs. Forget the elevator, she didn't have time for that. Cedro's other wife took the elevator, so Xyla beat her to the door.

Xyla opened the door and said, "Why, hello there. What can I do for you?"

"Praise be to the Exalter," Joraes, the worker, said. "Good mid-morning to you. I am just here to check your devices in the basement for operational performance and see if your energy cell is working properly."

Joraes was an average-looking guy Puerto Rican or maybe Cuban Knower. The way he spoke gave it away second to his features. His dark skin acknowledged that truth, along with his solid black hair and a very well-groomed goatee. His barber knew what he was doing. Joraes noticed his welcome seemed a bit prolonged.

Xyla was even happier than happy to help. "Oh sure, please follow me," she said as she stared flirtatiously into the crewman's eyes. She led him to the basement and then made her move: "So what is your name, anyway?"

"Joraes," he said, not even paying attention to her.

Xyla started her plan: "Joraes, don't you get tired of all this hard work?" It took mere seconds for Xyla to captivate this utility worker. She had spent days crafting this secret plan, and it was going perfectly.

Joraes liked where this was going, but he said, "Listen, the headmaster of this house hasn't authorized me to body share with you or anyone else in his household. You know how the process goes; it just won't work, lady."

"Oh, don't worry about all of that. I won't tell your secret if you don't tell anyone about mine."

Joraes had no idea he was being used, just like a bear tracked by a patient hunter. Joraes was a simple bear, wandering the routine of his day, not realizing someone was waiting to trap him and then use him as she saw fit. Why is it that people flinch on impulse of the now and never think out the consequences of the later?

The following weeks, Xyla had manipulated Joraes with her secret favors in order for him to build her a private room in the basement filled with an air supply, toilet, and a sound-proof hidden door. The prison bars from an abandoned jail were just a bonus to add the feeling of banishment. Joraes worked on the room until it was complete, and then, Xyla turned the tables indeed. Joraes came to the door as usual, but this time, Cedro answered the door.

"Oh, headmaster, I didn't expect to see you home at this time. Usually, your wives say you are at the gym doing your extensive workouts," Joraes said.

Cedro said firmly, "Xyla told me you made a pass at her in a way to lead to body sharing. I don't like what I am hearing here, Joraes. After all, you are so close to becoming a headmaster of your own house and given three wives, or husbands, if that's your deal."

"You would be out of this lowly division full of work and sweat," Cedro continued. "I would hate to have to rob a fellow brother of this honor by reporting this to the Exalter's global unit and have you punished in these serious times of questionable allegiances."

Joraes was figuring it out word by word as Cedro spoke and realized what Xyla did in order to use him and get rid of him. He was stuck now as well and couldn't talk about what he did and what he got for doing it. All answers would lead to punishment or, worse, death.

He gave the answer Cedro expected: "I understand, sir. This is the last time you'll see me here. I'll send another crewman here on the next visit. I apologize for any misunderstanding and thank you for your mercy." Joraes turned around and began walking down the pathway from the house.

Cedro was, at best, a chest-puffing jerk, and he wasn't going to let Joraes just be humiliated. He wanted to add insult to injury: "Look at you, man. There is no way you could have my Xyla. Like it would ever happen. You had just better stick to fixing pipes. Get outta here and don't come back."

Joraes rolled his eyes as he went back to his car across the street. He started up his vehicle and looked one last time at the house. There was Xyla in her master bedroom window. She was smiling as she looked right at Joraes. She put her left hand to her mouth, blew Joraes a kiss, and waved good-bye, smiling. Joraes just drove away from the house, thinking some not-so-nice names for what seemed to be a crazy lady, after he thought it through. Maybe that cage was to trap her own husband, or worse, it could have been him. Oh well, at least he felt better now to be rid of that situation.

Chapter 13

"I have never even seen this opening before," Cedro replied in a convincing voice.

"Cedro, I can't believe that you've never seen this room before, that you have no idea there is a small prison with a toilet and air pipes coming into it. And that you have no idea why a Derogate's clothing is left in this cell with the number 252 on it."

Cedro seemed to have the light switched on. "Wait a minute, did you say 252?" He grew angry. "Oh, Xyla ..."

Xyla wasn't just Cedro's nice-looking wife; she was also a thinker, an observer. The Exalter's government manufactured drugs for Knowers to use at their will. Of course, these drugs, wine, and other disorienting drugs were rationed. However, Cedro, using his connections, had also found a way to build an empire of his within his workless empire. In his level 1 Knower division, his life was spent just to indulge. For Cedro, that just wasn't enough. He wanted more Aeons, more drugs, and more pleasure. The Exalter gave everyone a monetary allowance of Aeons, and although it was enough, many wanted more.

During the beginning, Cedro just sold to the Knowers, but then he decided to add Derogates to the mix, as well. After all, the Derogates were the people making, packaging, and shipping these drugs. Anyone who wished to have more drugs or alcohol would contact his sources and pay for them with the new global currency, called Aeons. The Exalter put the Aeon into effect right when he took power. Beforehand, people were throwing their silver and gold in the streets. The hope was that those who could melt all the silver and gold would then bring carriers of food back into the towns after the profits were received from those who were fortunate enough to have the old cash on hand. Of course, that was before it was outlawed entirely to have such metals. The Aeon became a large-scale welfare system, where the new government decided that everyone was somewhat equal and should receive money. Level 1 Knowers didn't even work, but they made the same as those who did work, if you could call it that.

Cedro started small and then built up more faithful Derogates and Knowers on each side. He had Knowers and Derogates manufacturing his drugs and also shipping them in their spare time. He would have insiders forge numbers of transported drugs on shipping manifest sheets. His people unloaded a certain amount from each shipment; no one missed the drugs and booze, since no one even knew it was on the shipment. Besides, drugs and alcohol were not anything that Knowers took seriously. The more serious issues were those involving the Derogates.

So what was Cedro going to do when he someday amassed billions of Aeons? The answer was simple: He would continue doing what he already was doing: buying fancy cars, using drugs, indulging in women, and sleeping his life away. Then he would wake up and exercise to keep the physique that he enjoyed marveling at in the mirror. Through all these dealings, he had given his three wives more than other wives would get. His wives had close to unlimited amounts of money to shop, spend, and accessorize. This was all payment just to keep quiet; none of them were tempted, at least not until Xyla found a reason to be.

It was late in the afternoon; Xyla knew the time was right, as she had been waiting. "Hey, Cedro, we need to have a private discussion," she said calmly.

"Sure," he answered. "Go ahead."

"No, no, take me to your private room, so we can talk more freely."

Cedro's eyebrows arched as he turned around to lead the way. The private room was a hidden room in the house with schematics erased from the Knower records. It was all a part of Cedro's scheming. The room had untraceable old-school hardwired lines, sound-proof walls, and a high-tech network all, of course, in a hidden entrance.

After they went into the room, he asked, "Well, what is it, Xyla?"

"Cedro, you know I love you and that I am faithful to all of your dealings. However, I am increasingly tired of the attention you pay that filthy Derogate worker, June. I have decided that she doesn't need to work for us anymore, and as of now, she is gone. Don't worry. I have taken care of all the details; I'm just telling you so you won't look into this further."

Cedro's eyebrows creased in anger, and he snapped, "Yeah, right; you don't tell me what to do."

Xyla continued, despite his comment, "You are thinking to yourself right now that you will do what you want and that I am servant to you. However, before you turn that tone, remember who knows your secrets. Remember just what would happen if the Exalter found out what you are doing. Don't think that I wouldn't be rewarded as his first and only earthly wife for the faithfulness I would show to him."

His blood was boiling at her proposed betrayal with anger, and then a bead of perspiration started at his top hairline as he thought about the real-life consequences of his actions.

"Cedro, think about it," she continued. "And just in case you think it would be convenient if I had an untimely death right about now, let's just say I have arranged insurance. Upon my premature death, all your secrets would still be exposed. I have taken care of that. And trust me, you will never figure it out, even though you think women are just, well, stupid. Now, this small misunderstanding should not come between us. Let's continue on as we were and pretend none of this ever happened, as long as you do what I say and forget June. I will see you at dinner, then. I have decided to make you something special because today I am rather happy." Xyla gave him a soft kiss on the cheek and exited the hidden room through the tunnel.

Cedro just sat there and remained in shock at everything. He knew for sure that he fantasized about June. He just couldn't figure out why Xyla went to such extreme measures to first get rid of June and then blackmail him to stay out of it. He decided he had no problem just staying out of it. After all, if the Exalter found out, then he would be done for. If Xyla could go to such extreme measures for something he viewed as small, what would be next? He always knew she was manipulating, and he often enjoyed watching her pull her moves on people; it made him laugh. This time was different because now he was in a position he had never been in before. He had to obey Xyla out of complete fear. The five minutes he spent thinking about it settled it. She would be getting special treatment and an increase of Aeons in the form of cash. That was the safest decision at least for now.

Chapter 14

"Listen, Nicolai, Xyla blackmailed me, for reasons I can't share with you, or I would face certain death. She was jealous of our Derogate worker, June, because I wanted her. June had the identifiers of 252 on her clothing, so I know it's her clothes. I could tell Xyla hated whenever I paid any attention to June. I didn't care; I just kept doing it. She told me she was getting rid of June, and I wasn't to interfere. I knew there were protocols for dismissal and that the main Knower office had to be notified. I used trusted contacts to find out what I could. I learned that a level 2 division Knower drove to June's Derogate house and falsely accused her family of breaking of our laws. She probably persuaded them with a whole bunch of Aeons. That is all I know. I was so stupid. Just look at what happened to June, man."

Nicolai thought it over a moment. "Well, Cedro, it looks like Xyla is the only person who knows where she is. Right now, we are here to talk about you and Kiyana. If you see her even one more time, you will regret it, as I will make sure it is your last. Oh, maybe you think your little guardian will protect you from me, since the Exalter is giving all of us one. Well, unlike you, I spend my days doing actual work on computers, and I've given your guardian a special program. All I have to do is dial a number, and your guardian will be given evidence that you worshiped the false god; you will be instantly reported to the Triune. That's right, the Triune, the headquarters of the Exalter. You seem to be a magnet for blackmailers, huh? Well, I am telling you if you test me, you won't see another sunrise. Stay away from Kiyana or else. As for this hidden cell and your sick wife, well, that's your problem to deal with, buddy."

Cedro was speechless at hearing this, at the discovery of the secret cell, and now once again, his life was in the hands of somewhat else. He was already nervous about the illegal businesses he was running, and now there was another blackmail scheme that could lead to his death. Nicolai walked over behind Cedro, opened his clenched hands, put something in his right hand, and then closed it. With Cedro's head turned downward, he felt something thin being put in his hand tied behind his back. After grasping the object, he could tell it was a small knife.

"Now cut yourself free, Boy Scout, and you better close those doors, unless you want Xyla to discover what you have found." With that, Nicolai punched the codes to the basement window and exited Cedro's house.

Nicolai was surprised at himself, but not as surprised as Cedro, who wondered how this guy had his house codes. Kiyana wouldn't have told him. He was baffled at how this would be plain rule follower just threw a snowball in the face of his world.

Meanwhile, Nicolai had expected to be nervous after confronting Cedro. Instead, he felt confident that not only had he solved his problem, he did it with no blood on his hands. Nicolai drove home, pleased for this first time in many years.

Chapter 15

Moments before any of the people mysteriously vanished, Tyrisha was on her bed, looking at the great book (she didn't even know the real title of it). In the room, the light dimmed and then brightened. As she looked around, the room took on an overpowering white light. She became scared and curious all at once. Then she saw him. She saw a figure like a man dressed in white linen. Closer examination of his outline revealed a sword on his side and intricate metallic armor covered his forearms. A red sash ran around behind his back.

The majestic being spoke in many similar voices all at once to her. "Tyrisha, do not fear."

Tyrisha was pretty much paralyzed as she focused on this being; her eyes froze solid on his face. He seemed to fade away as she was wide eyed and still staring this image which was burned into her mind.

The room slowly faded from a bright white back to its original state. Tyrisha looked around as the scenery faded; she checked again where the angel had been standing, but he was gone. Tyrisha thought about how her mother had always told her that accepting the son was the way to heaven. She thought it was just a figure of speech. She knew the son died but had never seen the whole book. The parts of the book she had just spoke so highly of him. She acknowledged it in her mind, but that was it. This meant people had to ask the son to come into their hearts and forgive them of their sins. Some people had been praying to the Only like that. Everything she thought she knew had changed.

Tyrisha glanced around the room. It was completely the same, and she began following the instructions and left the house amongst the panic outside.

Chapter 16

"So what about you, um, let's see here, Janae Donovan? Are you going to accept the holy Exalter as your God, or do you prefer idolatry mixed with bars and imprisonment?" The level 2 division Controller read her name, and you could tell he was completely bored with all of it.

Janae had been found at her house on the day of the great disappearance. She was just sitting at home when the Knower brigade came in. She didn't put up a fight. She came home to a house filled with just piles of clothing on the floor. Her entire family was gone. Her thoughts consumed her thinking that maybe the Only was real, or just maybe the Exalter is real and destroyed her family. In his broadcasts from their radios, he had always warned that someday, it would be too late for all who oppose him. After hours of thinking it out, she had decided that the Exalter must have kept his words. If her parents and sister were right, then why had they died? None of it made any sense, and none of it felt right. She knew something was wrong; she was completely alone and felt helpless. Being out of the routine of forced slavery scared her. How about that? The harsh routine of forced work, rations, and poverty had become a source of safety for this outspoken complainer.

While looking out into space, Janae said, "I will pledge my allegiance to the holy Exalter and denounce the false god."

With that, she was taken into another room. There, she received the quick incision. The woman operating the device strapped her wrist in the molded armrest. It did hurt briefly and was more uncomfortable for the first week, but then she got used to it. She wouldn't even know it was there if she didn't need to use it so much. With a swipe of her hand, she could access doors, gain entry to buildings, and learn the new way of the Knowers. More importantly, she learned about the one they served. She walked on the same earth only in what seemed a new body.

This complex device admitted her into a brotherhood of acceptance, luxury treatment, and a feeling of belonging. She was identified by this device in her hand. It actually made her feel recognized to be a number. It meant she was something. She was a part of something. Someone assigned her a place, and now, it was her time to get out of the ghetto.

She was given the treatment, a place to stay, and a new book, said to be inspired by the Exalter. The book was called The Forever & Most Powerful. She was told that after two weeks of adaptation, she would be assigned to a headmaster as one of his wives. Of course, she was nervous, but she was all too excited to get into that situation so that she could block out the feelings of her former family.

Some thoughts tried to come in. Thoughts like, Where are they? Where did they go? Janae would work on her makeup or pluck her eyebrows, which was a new thing, in order to look her best. She seemed to drown herself in the new Janae, just to forget the old one. Before Janae knew it, she found a name tag in her mailbox with the name of her new household. The name on the card was "Nicolai Turner." She read the name tag and mouthed the name without speaking. She wondered if he was a good man or a bad man. It didn't matter to her then, because anything was better than that trash bag of a life she was living.

$\mathcal{C}$hapter 17

Leviticus was on the trail with fellow Derogates as they all fled their homes, and the once small comfort of stability they had in their life, which was family being there. Now, there was one of two types of families: those who lost people and those who did not. Leviticus just kept on feeling a slight shift of relief that in this time of turmoil, he didn't have to provide for his daughter and wife. After one whole week of traveling, stopping only to rest and eat, it seemed his traveling had come to an end. He saw a sight and remembered the rumors that talked of free Derogates. The folk tales mentioned a place with a waterfall that gives you protection. Leviticus didn't realize he would live the meaning of that story. At the bottom of this waterfall was a large river as far as the eye could see, surrounded by lush green vegetation. You couldn't tell whether any human life existed in and around this area. However, he followed the group as they all formed into a single unit line.

In front of him, people were walking right through and behind the waterfall. This was no cakewalk, either. As he entered the wide stream, reflecting a skewed image of his own face, he was surprised. The stream was more like a wave, as it seemed four feet thick, and the cave opened into an area only wide enough for two people to stand side by side. As he entered the cave, soaked, he was surprised to see energy cells being used in this secret place. Lights lined the walls and ceiling, along with powerful fans that made the idea of drying much friendlier than waiting for the natural. The thick rocky doors closed behind all the new entering Derogates. The doors were at least three feet thick, with six inches of lead coating the outer doors. This was a precaution to avoid infrared sensors that Controllers popularly used. They would also protect against the x-ray devices the Knowers used to peer through even thick buildings. It would be unlikely that such scans would even be attempted in such a desolate area. Deeper into this cave, a set of thick doors opened, and they all entered.

Leviticus thought to himself, *What? Get this, they are actually scanning us to see if we have any devices implanted in us to detect a would-be Knower ... Wow.*

After being scan by the armed guards, he entered the facility. Loudspeakers rang out with a man on the screen, who seemed to be staring right at you. He was a handsome black man. He looked old enough to be a well aged grandpa. He had the face of a man you would let command you.

He said, "New Derogates, former Knowers, and those of you who held no allegiance: forget the past, forget the slavery, and forget what they have called you. That word *Derogate* is forgotten here. You are now all called a NOVA, just like us. We are the *None Of Value Abandoned*. On the other side, many of you are the chosen ones left here on earth to make the great decision. So many people were caught up in offense and ignorance. But now, we have seen firsthand what our faith couldn't grasp. As a NOVA, our mission is first to find and shelter all those non-Knowers who were left behind. Two, we are to also gather our lost brothers and sisters who are Knowers who want to convert to serving the true God. Third, we are to protect ourselves from the Knowers as well as provide shelter, food, and water to sustain ourselves. Here, we put each other above ourselves. And by the way, we have full copies of the holy book, which most of you have never seen. We are going to have classes, teachings, and worship. In addition to all this, we have to accept that the 2,555 days of judgment are quickly passing. Welcome to your temporary home. We are grateful you are here."

Leviticus was having a hard time processing all this. How long had this underground secret city been here? How was it supplied? Who made it? How did they have Knower technology in place? Who would be brave enough to scheme such a revolt? The city seemed like a massive prison. There were areas of round dome-type living sections with thousands of residents. A straight path ran through one dome, and then you would enter another dome. It was ultimately the most impressive structure that Leviticus had ever seen. More importantly, he felt a sense of belonging, a sense of hope, and a sense of purpose; he felt like he would see Tyrisha and Zeneth again.

Above all of that, Leviticus could hardly grasp that such a nice place was available for him to stay in. He more or less pictured hiding in the wilderness in some dark musty cave.

Chapter 18

Nicolai was at home just relaxing by sitting down watching the news reports of all the chaos. Now, if only his mind could relax. A knock came at the door and he got up to answer it. A Controller was at the door with a woman dressed up like she was going to an upscale party.

"This woman is for you," the Controller said without any emotion. "The Exalter himself has sent this envelope, sealed for your viewing."

Nicolai was puzzled about this. He had what was called a stone age view of marriage, and he didn't want any more women. After all, this was the new age, where everyone wanted to erase the word morality from the dictionary and record books. He caught himself smirking as he thought about that new remake of the long-forgotten movie *Jurassic Park*. Jurassic times sounded good to him, compared to the present. Well, it would have been better just to bring back extinct ideology rather than man-eating monsters. He went into his living room and sat down to open the envelope. The seal was the Exalter's, all right. The envelope had the universal symbol that the Exalter used to seal envelopes with his signet ring. That symbol was everywhere with that silly point representing the whole world and those three lines showing the Exalter's

hierarchy, starting with himself at the top, naturally.
He opened the letter; it read:

> Nicolai, I have given you Janae as your wife.
> Remember I mentioned her to you after your
> impure contact with Tyrisha, the Derogate? Janae will
> fill the gap that you have in your life. As a new level one
> Knower, I expect you to take her as your fourth body
> sharing partner and show her our ways. I know that this
> new addition to your house will fill your soul, like you
> wanted to save Tyrisha. The fact is Tyrisha is gone, and
> now, you can save her friend, Janae, just as you wished
> you could save Tyrisha. Enjoy each other, and thank
> you for your obedience, my son. I love you very dearly.

Nicolai's eyes grew wide as he began to read. He couldn't believe
this new addition to his house. After all, none of his wives shared the
secret they all kept with outsiders. The secret was that at first, Nicolai
tried to go with the flow of what everyone else was doing. He had never
been intimate with his two other wives. He felt it just wasn't right. He
felt as if he would be cheating on Kiyana. Instead, they found love
elsewhere, and he just provided for them as he could while they kept
their mouths shut, happy about such freedoms.

Nicolai talked to Janae, who was sitting on a couch across from him;
no one else was home. "Listen, Janae, I'm done pretending. I already
have three wives, and the truth is, I only ever wanted one. That idea is
so old fashioned, I realize that. Now, I am sure you are a great person,
and you are indeed a pretty young girl. However, you will not find
intimacy from me. Instead, I can offer only my friendship. I know that
there are laws against what I am saying. However, I am guessing this is
your first assigned house, judging from the fresh incision mark on your
hand. It wouldn't be smart to mess things up. If you wish to seek body
sharing partners through the approval process, I encourage you to do so.
You can do whatever you choose. Please don't feel offended or upset. If
nothing else, you will be safe and not in fear here. Now, I have a spare
bedroom upstairs. It is the third door to the right, and it is yours. Please

join us tonight at six thirty for dinner. I want you at my table. I realize the harsh reality you have come from, and you are welcome here as long as I am here."

Janae was just shocked. At first, while Nicolai was talking, she felt like she was being dumped from some loser boyfriend. Now, she felt like dirt. At least, she didn't have to get all nervous about being abused behind closed doors.

She responded, "I'll go upstairs now and join you at dinner. Thank you for your honesty and your kindness."

She got up and couldn't believe she handled that so well. What she really wanted to say was, "What? You don't want me? Why? What is your problem, pal? Am I not good enough for you because I was a Derogate?"

She walked up to the room, which was red, with a full bathroom, and she marveled at thinking this huge room was hers to live in. Here was the start of her new life, and she still felt like she didn't belong. Was she destined to feel completely out of place, completely unfitting, and completely insufficient? At least for now, she relished in the room and the stuff she now could call hers.

Ch

Chapter 19

The Seer approached the holy Exalter sitting in his chair, overlooking the city as the Exalter sat with his hands folded. "All the arrangements have been made, my lord. The Controllers are out scouting for Derogate traitors, and the prisons have been reopened to house the unacceptors. The incision is worldwide; by the end of next week, the rest of our Knowers will have the mark. My lord, you have conquered the world already in this short time. I am impressed by all of your work."

"It's not enough," the Exalter shot back, squinting his eyes and clenching his jaw. "I want all those who would run away from worshiping me dead. I want them dead. I want those who deny me to have their heads cut off. Keep the ones in prison to build my temple. I will show them who the real king of Jerusalem is. I want it more glorious than Solomon's temple. This is my time, mine, and I have been waiting so long. All of us have been waiting a very long time on this miserable realm. The chaos will soon start, and they will look to me for answers and protection. I haven't completely received their full worship. Who would worship a god in a world where you have everything you want? There is no thankfulness in the flesh of men when life is easy. Striking their flesh will teach them respect and make them dependent upon me. I am their god, and they will worship me as their only and most high one."

The Exalter was pleased to hear himself speak. He was pleased to be at the top pillar, looking down at a game where he had arranged all the pieces. He knew which way the men and women would move. The Seer was a programmed robot (except for the fleshly body he lived in). He did everything that the Exalter wanted. He was the accuser of unbelievers, he was the voice for the Exalter, and he was the one who gave lectures on the new ways of living, according to Knower guidelines. The Seer himself had actually convinced himself that the Exalter was as good as God in the flesh. He also convinced the rest of the world the same thing he believed. He was called to be here for such a time as this. The Exalter's thoughts were anxious and shuffling. He had so much knowledge. He seemed to know the future. He knew what the outcome of everything would be.

The program, named Reborn, had been completed a month earlier. The Exalter had chosen three men to undergo the procedures. He wanted real men to oversee his global takeover. The Reborn program could have been described as the creation of steroid-pumped human guinea pigs. Neurologists were skeptical of the procedures, claiming the rapid cell and muscular growth would increase aggression and other negative emotions, such as rage. The Seer replied by demanding the scientists re-engineer the brain chemistry of the men to make them more subservient. As an extra measure, a blank chip was placed in each man as extra insurance, with the hope to keep them in check. When the blank chip was activated, the programmer could influence emotions through biological stimulants and suppressants. They would receive orders only from the Seer or the Exalter himself. No one knew anything about the men, not even their names. The Exalter had said that their old names were unimportant; only their new names mattered.

As predicted, the injections and rapid cell growth processes were successful. The process actually took a solid month, as the men had to sleep off the growing changes (the human body could not keep up with all the enhancements). It was almost like they really did have a new birth. They were kept in chambers almost like infants in the womb, undisturbed. The scientists were scared of what they were creating and joked nervously about how they were glad the three men were asleep.

The day finally came to wake them up.

The Exalter walked in without his Terafin guards, which was unusual. He told the scientists to initiate the consciousness stage and to then leave the room. Then half of the capsules were open, exposing the men to an array of warm mist, so they were not completely visible. As the machines began to make noises, the lights also changed, showing a sequence was being performed. All three men woke up. As they all sat up in unison, the normal response from a regular citizen would be to turn tail and run in panic. These men no longer looked like regular people. They looked like superhuman monsters made of bricks. They were similar to large concrete sculptures of massively muscular men made into real life. Two of them were around eight feet tall; the larger black man had piercing yellow eyes. He stood a head above the other two and couldn't make a regular man feel any weaker. The man on his left looked Caucasian, with blue eyes. The man on the right looked Egyptian. His eyes were amber brown. The remarkable fact about these monsters was that their pigmentation was brighter than usual, which made them impossible to ignore. The description might be called a shimmer.

The muscle mass of these men went beyond anything steroids could achieve. They had thick, large muscles, and the black man had the largest muscles of them all. The white man had the largest chest cavity, and the Egyptian's biceps looked like he curled bulldozers. The men looked out of control, like wild wolves, as they appeared to be pumped up and ready to exert fascinating energy.

The Exalter looked at them and said, "Stay where you are and listen."

All three men seemed irritated by the command, and their body language looked as if they were going to attack. Then something supernatural happened that no one witnessed at all (and for a reason, of course).

The Exalter simply said, "Take them."

At once, a wind whispered as some invisible force or multiple forces even came from behind the Exalter and attached itself to the three superhumans. They fell to their knees in pain and then rose again after a few seconds. Now, it appeared they were ready to listen under some other form of control.

He pointed to the tall black man, and the man stepped forward.

He spoke with precedence, "Forget all of your old names. You are now Tyranus." He pointed to the white man on the left. "You are now Granite." He pointed to the Egyptian on the right. "You are now Jupiter. Granite and Jupiter, you will report to Tyranus."

It was obvious that Tyranus would be the boss. He was the alpha. What a proper name he had. He looked like a predator for sure, and he could no doubt kill a Tyrannosaurus with his bare hands.

"Granite, you will cover all the territory of the west. Jupiter, you will cover all of the territory of the east. The goal of your new creation is to restore order and create stability in these times of rebellion against those who would choose to not worship me. They will even worship you. We have talked about this for a very long time. You all understand what I mean. Install fear into men so that they obey; you will reign over them and show them that I am not a god to be reckoned with. Now, my sons, there are men outside waiting to brief you and fix you up with the armor you will wear."

Like controlled zombies, they walked out the especially tall doors. Everything would need to be customized in order for these giants to travel. They each had their own custom-built air and land vehicles. The design for these men called for a new bone structure that was close to unbreakable. They were designed to never get sick, to not have any weaknesses, and to not need anyone's help. Their skin was easily bulletproof. These men relied on twenty-four-hour injections that were full of top-secret compilations. They were superhydration- and super-calorie-infused injections with a time released glycemic distribution formula. Of course, they were completely engineered for these men and ensured that they never felt weary or weak.

Chapter 20

It was all over the news and had been running all day. Mini war zones had broken out all over the globe. Mass storage containers of trash were piling up around the whole world. The government owned corporation Off The Globe had halted space shuttles of mass trash to outer space. Countless Derogates were not around to do the dirty work. Most Controllers demanded extra supplies and food rations on transports. Nicolai knew this problem was only a matter of time and figured that the Exalter would have this under control. After all, he was supposed to know how it all went, right? But it still didn't make sense because before the great disappearance, the Derogates did all the production work such as farming, harvesting, and also packaging food. They even shipped the stuff out while the Knowers just sat back, lazy; instead of supervising, they needed some supervising. And now the whole world was in trouble because of lost Derogates, fleeing Derogates, Derogates that became Knowers, or Derogates that were now in prison being held for whatever reason.

The news anchor continued, "The death toll in Texas has surpassed those of China, now at 642 deceased. According to Derogate investigations, this morning at 11:30 a.m. Central Standard Time, worldwide communication centers were reporting shortages on regular shipments. As military outfits received this news, they began to panic. Ships and containers were hijacked by armed Knowers. Reports of the rebellion Derogates were also coming in, although not as large as Knowers attacking Knowers. Ships returned to ports in China and elsewhere with stolen supplies, and further violence ensued. Many believe this is a direct result of the harsh drought that is being experiencing globally. The holy Exalter has not commented on the shortage of supplies. It is not known who sent these radio communications or if in fact the statements of shortages are even true."

Wow, of course that drought was going to create problems in relation to water and food. It had been the strangest thing most people had ever seen. Where were the clouds, anyway? Ever since a month ago, when the Exalter basically started taking over the world, the drought came right after. Meteorologists might have well as never gone to school. No one had an explanation for why there were no clouds and why there hasn't been any rain going over four weeks now.

Great, what was Nicolai going to do now? The world around him was falling apart. He couldn't help but think of back a short time ago, when none of this even existed. First, the wives and the separation of believer and nonbelievers. Second, all the rules and ridiculous lifestyles of the lavished lazies. Third, a system seeming to slowly funnel into a huge controlling grip, where everyone would be held at gunpoint, for who knows what? Finally, there was a shortage of supplies, and people were starting to act crazy; they were scared they might not have enough food. He shook his head and rolled his eyes, as if he had seen this coming.

Well, actually, he did see it coming. His position at the Knower offices gave him access to transactions in many different fields. He predicted that the output would slow down after the confusion of the great disappearance, and there was no one to replace the Derogates. It was forbidden for any of the Knowers to go out and do some real work, instead of just holding weapons and wearing armored suits for show. How can you sustain yourself when everything you need is controlled? There is no way to stock up, and even if you could, what would you do when it ran out? There would be no other source for it.

Nicolai went to bed that night rather nervous. Somehow, at the same time, it didn't matter, anyway. His thoughts continued to ramble as he lay down in an empty bed. Kiyana was probably mad that Cedro wouldn't see her, and she might have figured out Nicolai was to blame. He didn't even know if she was in the house. But it didn't seem to matter. Even though he would wake up, go to work, come home, and try to spend time with Kiyana. He may have done all that on purpose, but it was all without much meaning anymore. If the world did fall apart, he, all in one sense, didn't even care. What was he going to lose? A broken, now four-partner marriage, when he only wanted one woman? His job had little meaning to him, which was now just a routine to get out of the way and over each day. He didn't even really buy all this holy Exalter mind control, like the rest of the trained zombies did. So what if he acted like it, even to the Exalter's face? So what if this guy did all these earthly miracles and got peace? So w-h-a-t? That didn't make him God. The lifestyle that this Exalter set up had no purpose of gaining wisdom, learning, or even progressing in any way that he could see.

Just then, a team of Controllers and the Derogate police unit kicked in the door at Nicolai's house. The specialized team began to sweep through Nicolai's house in the dark, as the energy cell had been turned off. He frantically jumped out of bed and grabbed a flashlight. He opened up a cabinet and pushed several buttons, releasing a hatch and revealing another layer of the closet underneath. He flipped another switch, which enabled a mini energy cell that fed power to the screen he was now looking at. The long vertical screen was under glass and displayed cameras lit up in the whole house. He spoke quickly after opening up the secret cabinet and said, "Audio."

He was thinking to himself in between the motions, I do more than sit at a desk all day. These people don't know who they are dealing with.

After the audio came on, Nicolai opened a small section of the screen and pulled out a surge displacer. This non-lethal handgun fired over one thousand rounds, and one round was good enough to stop a mountain lion. This type of weaponry was no joke. A blast from this device would hit its target and spread out all over the body, looking like they were covered in a lightning force field. After that, the victim would hit the pavement, completely unconscious and rather foggy.

The audio was unclear, and then after a moment, the mic zoomed in on one of the masked men; he said, "The first floor is clear. Target is most likely on the second floor. Switch to grazers."

Nicolai's eyed widened; he knew what grazers were. They were like the old-time bullets but released chemical agents directly into the bloodstream; this meant he had been marked for painful extermination. He watched as they started up the stairs. He hustled over to the door and looked to the left. A faint shadow in the dark showed a body almost to the top of the stairs.

Nicolai quickly lined up his shot. *Zuupt. Zuupt.* The second blaster shot attached itself to the first controller and took him down, as the other men behind him on the stairs watched. He knew he had nowhere to hide in the house. He wasn't prepared for something like this, at least not yet. He ran down the hall and turned right, slamming the door open to Janae's room. She sat up and screamed, completely terrified; she had no idea what was going on. Nicolai had his mind made up as he picked up speed. He ran for the window and crashed through it. He was airborne and landed on his side lawn. The air whished through his ears as he looked toward the dark grass, hoping he could survive the fall unscathed.

Thud. Nicolai's shoulder and hip bone took the brunt of the fall from his bed and forced him painfully awake. He was sweating, and for a few seconds, he couldn't tell if he had been dreaming or was dreaming now. He got up and went to the chest cabinet. It had not been open, and the power was on. He went to his bathroom, turned the water on, and rinsed the sweat off his face with some cool water. He realized that it was just a dream, but he felt deeply disturbed. He never had such a vivid dream that was so real, leaving such an impression on him. He walked to the bedroom window and looked down.

Kiyana was down there, talking to a Controller officer.

He spoke, "Code 258. Audio, zoom in front porch."

The speaker came out of the wall, and he had an ear to the conversation. Nicolai wasn't paranoid. He considered himself prepared. In this case, it proved to be a life-saver.

"Yes, ma'am, I have everything down in the report. I have not talked to Cedro about any of this but will report the alleged blackmail that you claim your headmaster is using on him. It is noted that your headmaster is not praying to the Exalter, giving thanks to our holy leader, or acknowledging his rules as law. I will also add that he is not fulfilling his body sharing duty at home with any of his wives. This behavior is suspicious, and as cautious as these times are, there are no taking chances. I must also tell you that because of the work your headmaster is involved in, he is a person of interest due to the information he has been exposed to. Be very careful and mention nothing of this. Protocol will be followed, and this information will be reported directly to Triune headquarters. Do you understand everything I am telling you?"

"Yes, of course, Officer. Thank you so much for your time. I will be careful; you don't have to worry about that."

Nicolai's eyes had squinted in hatred and clenched his jaw during the tail end of this conversation. He was infuriated; maybe his dream wasn't as coincidental as he thought. It all seemed too ironic: that the one person he had cared about just betrayed him.

Speaking in a slow, callous voice, he spoke out, "Audio off."

Chapter 21

The US Military Knowers, now called Circle soldiers, were getting used to their new names, along with the rest of the world. The Circle soldiers had the same emblem as the Exalter's symbol. The emblem looked like an incomplete circle. An arrow was at the gap in the circle. In the middle were three horizontal lines, which stood for the Exalter, the Seer, and the Exalter's spirit. It was told that the Exalter's spirit was on the Terafin guards. And everyone knew the story where a madman had used a sniper rifle to shoot some of the Terafins. They seemed to die, but then, they miraculously healed right on everyone's halovision. Some were skeptical and claimed it was all a setup, but others were sold. It didn't matter if it was Derogates turning themselves in, Knowers, or rebels. The Circle soldiers had authority over them all and would give out food if it was there. It was the worst when the people would work a full day and then were told the rations hadn't arrived yet. It was not an easy time for anyone's rumbling stomachs.

"Why we waitin' 'round here in all this silence?" a soldier named Smith said. "Somebody pinch a fart or somethin'. I'm getting tired of the quiet."

Smith kept his stubbly face straight as he cracked yet another joke. The boys were used to it. He was predictably divorced, in his thirties, and considered himself a plain Idaho man. These days, Smith's face was tan, but the rest of him was pretty much ghost white. He had a way of keeping his face straight when making jokes that left people rolling in laughter. He loved to make this face that said, "Whaaat, you're not serious?" with those downward eyebrows and ridiculous smile. He kept his same look of wearing boots with his pants tucked in them and loved smoking cigarettes basically all the time. Most of all, he found live worth living by telling jokes and combing his medium-length brown hair. He wasn't much of a tough guy with his scrawny build, and he knew it. It didn't matter that would just be good joke material.

In the bunker, five Controllers waited as they were deployed from the states to the northeast tip of Kazakhstan, right on the border of Russia. Their assignment was to control local militia of either Derogates or Knowers who tried to steal any cargo being transported by roadway.

Rodriguez started in, "Man, what are we gonna do besides sit and wait? We gonna start in on all that religious babble we bring up when nothing else is there?"

It was pretty much common knowledge about the past religions, although the new generation didn't know anything. So many years ago, society worshiped the outlawed Only, and during that time, that religion was all but overthrown by those who followed any other kind of god. Members that took on violent religions were now just like the rest: working as a servant or converting to worship the Exalter. With all of that history of religious wars, it was ironic to think nothing had changed from past to present.

Rodriguez was a twenty-six-year-old Puerto Rican who loved his heritage, especially his past outlawed religion, and his family. He stood a good bit over six feet tall with a decent build and tattoos of different things on this back and arms; the guys teased him about trying to show them off. When he spoke, he could not hide his accent. He had a tendency to sing in Spanish on the walking missions; some days, it was nice to hear, and on others, it wasn't. He would sing in times where singing didn't fit the tone. It must have been a coping mechanism. Rodriguez had a beautiful señora at home and was eager to get back to her. He was always in a good mood, but talk bad about him or his family, and those were fighting words. Rodriguez also didn't like slackers. His idea of a good day was to have accomplished something. That made him feel whole.

Fields pitched in next; he said, "I'm just saying, guys, consider it. We've been protecting each other's backs for years. We've been in the middle of nowhere many times, but we don't know what each other really believes. I mean, heaven forbid if anyone dies, but I'd like to know how to honor someone, you know? We all know what the Exalter's law is; centuries ago, my family's heritage was mostly Jewish."

Fields was the kind of person who said what he was thinking while working, but he was respectful about it. Not too long ago, he had been married with a little one back home. He looked like a typical dork bomb defuser, with his glasses. It was a mystery to the boys why he even wore those dumb things; LASIK correction was free to Circle soldiers. Fields felt that he was made that way and wanted to accept who he was, even if he didn't have perfect vision. His hair was like an old-time TV anchorman, complete with combover. He was clean shaven and was the cleanest cut in the group, even with his language. Sure, he was sensitive, all right. He was made fun of as a kid, but enlisting was something he could be proud of and a way to provide for his family. Fields had a kind and warm smile to offer to anyone who would receive it.

Morgan interrupted in his deep voice, saying, "Yeah, let's talk about Porter's old family past. Out of all the people in the world, how can only 144,000 to go to heaven? Hmm, you got better odds playing the lottery, kid."

After Morgan said that, he took a relaxed drag from his cigarette. He didn't care about anything at this stage of his life. He had been through enough pain to justify that, he felt. He had a rough life, searching for purpose and answers to all the questions of living. He was smarter than most people. He could figure things out faster, think quicker, and work better. At age thirty-five, he had experienced more pain in his life than some do in two bad lifetimes. But his ridiculous amount of knowledge made him depressed. You could tell a guy about something and he seemed to know how the story would end. Who would think some guy from Indiana knew so much? Smith gladly threw out jokes about how Morgan knew all there is to know about corn crop watching, usually with no response.

Morgan had been heartbroken by a small handful of women in his lifetime. Years went by and he only let out that many of those bad relationships gone bad were the fault of his own hands. Well more specifically, the fault was from his words is what he gave away. It must have been what he said to people. He had suffered a life shattering and deep betrayal with in his family that he would not talk about. He didn't say it but it was obvious the feelings he had felt; abandonment, pain, hatred, and a numbness. Whatever he was going through he suffered every day in silence. Despite all his knowledge, he couldn't find happiness, even with an admirable woman by his side waiting back home. The very thing he longed for was the thing he knew he couldn't have. Maybe it was his impatience or that hidden temper. He was effortlessly handsome and had that look of a handsome old cowboy you might find on a cigarette pack. He would drink if it was available to hide the pain, but he never talked about his personal life with his men.

Porter snapped, "Shut up, man; it's none of your business what my family used to believe in. Everyone's belief system changed five years ago, so I don't know why you babies are whining about it now."

Porter was very sensitive about his family background. After all, few black families used to be in that religion. The whole thing was embarrassing. When he grew up, he never told the crew he hung out about such stuff, and it was a mistake to share it with these guys. Porter lived thirty-six years; his life started in poverty and negative memories. His much-loved father finally got a job with the rising government and was home every night after working in an office building. It was a far cry from those seasonal jobs he used to get. Porter's mom could finally stop working at those lowly jobs and stayed home. After enduring hard times, they became a very tight family.

Porter was twelve when the quality of their life picked up, but it was hard to get away from the pool of bad influence he called friends. It was hard until they moved away to that gated community, and then it was easy. Porter faced his own challenges, still feeling poor from that pain, but it wasn't like that now. Now, he was doing like his dad did and working for his family. His father had tried to talk him out of enlisting and even offered him money and a job, but Porter wanted to serve his country. He wanted to make a difference.

Fields chimed back in, "That's the whole point; we all used to have different religions, and now it is just one because someone told us to and shows up with all of these powers. We are just doing what we are told to. Ohhh good doggies… meanwhile, the world around us is falling apart. Some control and peace from that miracle treaty. Break it down for me, Morgan. You are the one who studied all of this mumbo-jumbo. I want to hear what you have to say. We all know this talk is illegal, yeah, sure, but c'mon, so I can just get it over with and sort it out in my head."

Morgan took a couple puffs on his cigarette; an outsider would have thought he didn't know he was being addressed. But that was Morgan's character: to think and speak only when it was important. Out of the whole bunch, he seemed to be the toughest and the calmest. He studied all that theology stuff and also worked demanding manufacturing jobs before being selected to be in the Knower military, and he was well respected, even if he was more blunt than most. Morgan acted like he couldn't be killed, and stranger, he didn't seem fearful of death at all.

Smith didn't wait a second to pipe in a smug remark: "Awesome, and it's not even Wednesday, but at least I can be a part of some illegal, blasphemous Sunday school. Best go wax my guillotine while we are at it. I don't want my blade getting stuck halfway down. Imma need a clear cut you know? I don't want them to have the fat guy sit on it to finish me off."

That was just like Smith: always the funny guy with a smug comment. That was the part he played. Smith was ready to add his part in this.

"Well, I for one grew up Catholic, and you all know I was spoon-fed that ideology, and yeah, as a kid, I thought I had to pray to Mary. Pshhht, what a tool man. Oh well, the point is Fields is right, man. I would like to know about the other religions that used to be. Why not? Because someone said we can't talk about it. We are chained down by those restrictions, while we fight for other's freedoms that we'll never know about."

Morgan tossed his cigarette filter on the ground and said, "You all know that I keep what I think all bottled up inside. But I will tell you: Something stinks about all this. Too many things are coming together; my studies lead me to believe in something different than this. As far as religion goes, yeah, I do have to say that I think they got it all wrong.

Jehovah's Witnesses don't know what to believe. They misinterpret the 144,000 in the forbidden book; it was the branches of the tribes of Israel, but somehow they changed it into the number of people who will enter heaven. They don't believe in the main concept of the forbidden book, which none of you even know about."

All three of the men's eyes widened, and their ears perked up because this kind of talk was unlawful, and they didn't know anyone who even laid eyes on the forbidden book.

"The Witnesses don't believe in a Holy Trinity, which the book clearly states is the true God (also called the Only by Derogates), his son, and the spirit, which was given to all men upon the sacrificial death of God's son. Those who ask for forgiveness in the son's name are granted pardon and a ticket to heaven, if they are lucky enough to be the select 144,000 that make it to heaven. The Witnesses don't recognize the son; instead, they regard the son as less powerful than the father and not the true son of God. For the life of me, I can't understand how different religions have the same book and can make complete nonsense out of plain English."

You could tell those were fighting words to Porter. He stood up and pushed his bulky chest out, but Fields motioned for him to calm down and just take a seat. Porter exhaled, shaking his head as he sat back down.

"The old Catholics, in most cases, are a mixed-up bunch as well. They give the glory to a woman named Mary in the forbidden book; they say she carried God's son in her womb through divine intervention, without any sexual conception. Some even end their prayers in her name, but according to the forbidden book, they should be saying, 'in the name of God's son.' The son's death is like a connection for believers to get to the father from his sacrificial death. Forgiveness is given freely through God's son's death. Catholics believe that God speaks through the old Catholic church and the former pope, whom you all know the Exalter killed. However, the forbidden book teaches that the book is the word of God, not teachings from other religious leaders trying to act like they are God, speaking in flesh. Catholics also believed that they have to perform good works in order to get in good with the church and God, whereas the forbidden book does not teach this gets you to heaven. Yet some also end prayers in the son's name and accept the son at face value so again one religion with different branches."

Rodriguez piped in, "I don't know where you got your info from, papi, but you shouldn't talk about the holy mother that way. Just because I claim to be a Knower doesn't mean that our family doesn't still hold on to the old ways of thinking."

Morgan kept his head down until after Rodriguez finished speaking.

"The Mormons also disagreed with the old Christians," Morgan continued, "who are now what you all know as Derogates. That's right, Derogates … The Mormons believed that the son of God was not birthed by divine intervention, but that it was a natural birth. They also believe that the father, son, and God's Holy Spirit, also called the trinity, are not so like the Christians believed. They believe them to be distinctly different; they are three separate gods. You can forget all that because, stupidly enough, according to one man who started the religion, he made his own book for the religion, and yet he believes also in the forbidden book, as long as it is translated correctly. Well, that man must be blind because his own testimony contradicts the forbidden book he followed. The forbidden book says that anyone who adds to the forbidden book will be condemned to hell, so there you have it: every one of his followers down the hell chute. In addition, they believe good works are the ticket to heaven and don't accept the son as the way to salvation."

All the men in this falcon sweep unit jerked their necks back and made faces in disbelief that Morgan was condemning a group of people to hell so easily. They each began looking around to see what the other was thinking sizing up the facial expressions.

Smith was the only person not taking offense. Instead, he had twisted his lips into a smile and did his signature eye roll.

"And I betcha none of 'em even once took a step to study any of it; like the rest, they opened their mouth, happy to swallow the pills asking for more. The other outlawed religions have disagreeable points as well. They all disagree with if the son was truly the son of God or just a prophet, if the son actually died or just ascended into heaven, and they all think that good works will gain you a spot in heaven. In any case, we all believe everyone else has the interpretation wrong. And then, a large majority never claimed a god or something to worship. If you can believe it, they just thought they should live a certain way. That means finding a place of peace, understanding, and right in their own eyes. And can you believe that even those who believed in the Only made their own man created branches called denominations, with different petty beliefs creating their own separations that their so-called God never asked them to do? Hmm ..."

All the men sat there and just took it in. Morgan spoke slowly enough so they all could take it in. Morgan took out another cigarette and lit it up. It was as if he needed to grab a smoke because he had unloaded a huge burden from his thoughts. He could never share those thoughts with anyone without being killed for treason. But he felt them every day and for so long.

Porter thought about how he felt insulted but at the same time enlightened, considering he never studied any of that. Rodriguez sat there, and if it had been anyone else, he might have gunned him down, but Morgan was Morgan. He wondered why Morgan seemed to know so much, and even put down some religious beliefs, but he didn't take one on his own. He then wondered how many people just believe what their parents tell them to and accept that as fact, just because. Smith didn't care about any of it. Sure, he listened to it all and took the considerations. However, in his eyes a real god would know everything and judge a man as the man was and then decide his own fate. So really for Smith, he just made God to be whatever his mind thought he would be, according to him. Fields, on the other hand, was intrigued and wanted to consider all points as he thought it through.

Morgan was never extremely chatty, and bringing up a subject twice could prove to be irritating, so Fields started, "Morgan, two things interest me about what you said. Don't take offense to anything I say when I go this route. But you spoke about the forbidden book as if you favored it and actually believed it. I mean, you acted like you thought some of those belief systems had it all wrong and kinda like the Derogates were right. I wonder why. I also wonder why you gave a name of God and calling something else the Holy Spirit, and even Mary, but you gave no name to God's son. Is he just named God's son, then? I don't get it."

"First thing I'm gonna tell you is, don't think that those with different religions in the past didn't spit on each other's beliefs behind their backs. Let's get real here. If I believe in a creator you don't, yes, I'll think you're wrong and throw you in the idiot bucket. I'll either feel pity for your ignorance or dislike you. And don't think there aren't plenty of chumps out there pretending to be Knowers who are planning their own religious takeover. We saw first-hand how violent the East religions were becoming."

Morgan didn't want to play preacher role, but he felt the need to say his peace about it anyway, despite what others thought, how offended they got, or whatever else. After all, people were dying, and this stuff was coming true in front of his very own eyes, even if these ignorant comrades next to him had no clue.

He began, in a serious voice, "I favor the forbidden book because I read it. I read it all, boys, despite all the historical burnings you heard about. And after reading it and seeing all that is going on, it is like seeing the future come to play, just as the book said it would. So is it coincidence that some book can predict things that are going on now? I will leave that cup for you all to drink. But make no mistake: If I am right, we are all in for some hell on earth, and then this life will end and another one, good or bad, will begin. As for the name of God's son, he is called Jesus, and you buncha wide-eyed little girls better never repeat that name again. But if things go south like I think they will … Well, then, you had better call to that name, cuz ain't no one else gonna save ya."

Morgan took another drag from his cigarette and then threw it on the ground; he stomped it out with his boot and then walked away without another word. Morgan was back to solitude. He would return to his unit named Falcon Sweep. They always had a two part mission; obey and execute.

Chapter 22

Leviticus sat down on a bench and looked around at the secret indoor city where he now hid. How was it that he felt so safe in that place amongst all the turmoil going on outside these walls? The energy cells in this place were magnificent. The light they displayed could make you feel as if you were really outside instead of man-made sunlight.

A young man strutted over and took a seat next to Leviticus on a bench. He barely noticed the man, as he was taking in the scenery of trees and landscaped greenery around him. Never had he been able to relax in such an environment.

He laughed inside as he thought to himself, *Mud slop ginger bread house.* It was an expression he used to say to Tyrisha when she was a child as he made his own bedtime story, making fun of their home.

"What do you think of it here?" the young man next to him asked.

Leviticus turned his head to the right to see who was talking to him. The young black man was in his lower twenties and looked healthy and vibrant. This young man had a unique skin tone and it actually looked neat. His hair was shaved short, his eyes were dark but warm, and he seemed very tall and limber.

Leviticus replied, "I think it feels better in here than out there, but without my daughter or my wife, I feel pretty empty."

The young man replied, "Well, sir, I somehow feel confident that you will see them soon and that all will work out for you. Don't give up now. You made it here, didn't you? I'm Talique. So tell me, what's yours?"

"My name is Leviticus."

Talique's eyes grew wide. "That is an interesting name. How do you suppose you got it?"

He gave him a strange look and answered, "I'm guessing my parents liked it."

"Well, Leviticus, I think your name is more important than you know. Names mean something, you know? My father is Samuel Alleo, and he and I are both descendants of the man who started building this place."

Leviticus found himself somewhat intrigued. "So tell me, Talique, if your family built this place and believed that this great disappearance would take place, then why are you here talking to me?"

Talique smiled and shot back, "I had to blend in this world with everyone, keeping track of everyone. I mean, we all did. I had the mark on my hand. Do you see the scar from where it was removed? The truth is, I believe that mark kept me from being taken. I thought before, when I grew up, that I believed. Then I became a part of that system out there. I began to be persuaded by my surroundings. I wanted to belong to that group of deceived people, and I knew I was being trapped but thought it would work out. Anyway, after all the people disappeared, all of our family had that secret plan. The bad part is I was the only one with the incision, and my family is gone. That recording you saw when you came in was my father, who made it before the great disappearance. It's sad and nice to see him, all at once."

Leviticus listened sympathetically to Talique.

"I just know that ever since everyone disappeared, I feel somehow peaceful about my eternal destiny if you will. Don't ask me how; it's just something that I feel inside. I feel like the Only is going to take care of me, and I know he will take care of you too. And I have vowed to do whatever it takes to get those who serve that false god the Exalter to come to know the Only."

Leviticus thought this young man had some wisdom for his age. He replied slowly, "Talique, it seems like you are on the right track, and I am glad I met you."

Talique leaned to his right and picked up a book. He turned back to Leviticus and said, "Here, I want you to have this."

Leviticus took the book with his left hand and read the title: "The Holy Bible? What's this supposed to be?" he asked skeptically.

Talique stood up and answered, "It's what they didn't want you to have. It's what they told you was outlawed, outdated, and no longer teachable. It is the answers to all the deception in this world. It's why the world wanted you to be chained down by time, work, and hard ship so you had not time for larger thinking. And here, you can read it with no fear."

He smiled without showing any teeth, bowing his head slightly. Then, he just turned around and just started walking away, disappearing into the sea of people, staring all around the underground city like vacationing tourists.

Chapter 23

Meanwhile, above the ground, conditions were still bad. Looking around, you might conclude that the earth had started spinning backward because everything was in confusion, despite this brand-new "almighty" ruler. The world just seemed poisoned. Many new diseases were arising from common animals that people were exposed to. New cases of infectious strains were found in cows, pigs, chickens, birds, and even domestic animals such as cats and dogs. Hospitals were being overcrowded with people experiencing flu-like symptoms with vomiting and diarrhea. Each strain seemed to be different, depending on how it was contracted. Many people were infected through eating contaminated meat, despite cooking it thoroughly. Others were simply exposed to the same breathing quarters or even by physical contact. The news seemed to come in continually. Just when the public thought they had enough, more bad came. It was like being ship wrecked on floating cargo pieces and more and more punishing waves kept hitting you. The previous conditions of the drought and lack of food left people all over the earth feeling stressed. However, they forgot who else needed food.

On one particular day, Max, an undistinguished Knower, was walking home from a visit to a colleague four castles down the street. Max thought he was a hardcore gangster. He was closer to a high class snob than a gangster. He was also more naïve than he should have been, at the age of twenty-four. He thought he knew it all. He wasn't the type of saggy pants gangster, either. He was a white guy with a thin chinstrap beard who thought he was intimidating, the kind of guy people would joke about after they passed in walking. Max wore the only legal metal left to wear, and that was aluminum. He would polish his glass earrings, necklaces, and bracelets he had made himself. Max liked to wear ballcaps and always made his best attempts at ghetto slang in conversations. By some, he was accepted, but others completely shunned him. He had just finished talking about how his household and his Knower friend would come together during this time of issues and try to help each other. Max's real plan was most likely to knock off his friend if it came to it and take his wives and also his leftover food supply and whatever else he could scavenge. Max didn't care about anything but Max. He didn't care about all the terror around him, and he didn't care about the Exalter. He was one of the few who realized a heavy wave of electromagnetic interruption would cause a malfunction in his guardian protector's system, putting him in a coma. On this particular day, he had powered down his protector: a mistake, for sure. He didn't care if there was some great creator known as the Only or not. Nobody was going to keep tabs on him.

Besides to him most people were fat, lazy, or stupid (and some were all three). He convinced himself he was master of his own world, where he had all the answers. In fact, he had told people in his own voice, "I would rather burn in hell for eternity than worship some god that demands I serve him. If he were a god, he would have known that I would never serve him, so why would he create me in the first place, just to burn in hell? And this god allows the diseases, famines, and murders to continue? Cheyah, right."

Max was on his way home, walking as usual with his chest puffed out and a face that said, "I'm tough. Whut, you don't think so? Come find out … Just come find out."

In the middle of this entire tough-guy thinking, Max began to trip, and he jerked his head up just as a mountain lion swiped its right paw at him, and he stumbled downward, face first on the sidewalk. Max, with all his tough thoughts, never stood a chance. As the big cat held Max's neck, waiting for the breathing to stop, the lion thought about how he had doubted his own survival until he finally found some easy food. That prey was Max, who had so many plans that came to an end in a way he never thought. The cougar dragged his body into the green spruce trees surrounded by crunchy and dead grass. The trail of blood on the sidewalk drew crowds of insects, which were also thirsty for survival.

Max's story was just one of many reports that were coming in. There were violent attacks by numerous animals, and many citizens had been killed. Even small packs of coyotes and stray dogs were forming alliances to stay alive. What else were they going to do? Many people had just let the dogs out of the house for good when there was no food to give them. All the animals had lost their fear of humans. Now they were in a world where a buffet was all around them. There had been issues of food before with so many animals, but why now were they killing humans? It just didn't seem right. It didn't seem to make sense; something was very definitely off. Once they stopped feeding animals manmade food, they made man the food.

*C*hapter 24

Something was also definitely off with Nicolai's life. His own wife, Kiyana, couldn't have made him feel more unloved, more uncared for, and more unvalued. The night he saw for himself that Kiyana had betrayed him, he almost had expected it. When you feel like everything is awful, more bad news will never surprise you. Ever since the Exalter came around, bad news and then some more bad news came into Nicolai's life. Everyone around him clapped like clueless penguins, happy to endure the new rules and the separations that took place. His one true wife, who shared years of solo enjoyment with him, had just turned into some brainwashed robot. He had to face it. He didn't know her anymore. She wasn't the same Kiyana he first fell in love with. Her face was like a reflection of a lost memory. He only had a mental picture, along with the memories held in his heart. As for the castle, he was the headmaster. As for the nice car, the Knower government job, and all the possessions, well, he couldn't care less about them.

Nicolai did take quite a while to fall asleep that night after witnessing Kiyana's betrayal. However, human instinct kicked in, and he realized he had to make a choice. The first choice would be to accept the fact that he was now exposed and face the legal consequences of meddling in Knower affairs, blackmailing under false pretenses, and breaking

Knower laws. That would most likely mean a blade falling down on his neck. Choice two would be to flee. Where do you flee as a Knower, though? That was all there was around him. He didn't want to think about it, but he knew his choice was clear. He was going to have to find these renegade militia or the hidden Derogates and join them.

Time for surgery, Nick, he thought to himself.

He took out the fine razors he kept in his red toolbox and opened the plastic casing to expose what did indeed look like surgical blades. He cut into the anatomy of his right hand as easily as he could in order to cause the least pain but also to accomplish his concentrated mission. Slowly but surely, the incision was starting to come out, along with some of his blood. The slender metal chip reflected in the bathroom light as he took it out. There were numbers across the small chip, just like everyone else's. Of course he had to get it out. After all, he could be tracked if he left it in.

At the same time, Nicolai was making his life more dangerous, as these incisions were used to track and scan citizens, open doors, and also get into public places. Then again, he wasn't that dumb, either. He had what he called a dummy incision. That's right: a chip that hadn't been assigned to anyone yet, and yes, it was functional. He would glue it onto his hand and cover it with a band-aid. He put some super glue on that would dry in less than ten seconds and a coating of Kiyana's makeup concealed the removal. Nicolai felt pretty good about what he had done, and he felt good to go against the grain in this situation.

He wore an angry face as he thought about where he was going to place the freshly taken out chip. He packed what he could carry and left for work at his normal time, in his normal clothes, looking like everything was normal. The even nicer part was that all his housewives were still asleep. Nicolai finished his coffee and said out loud, "They don't get out of bed until the day is half over, anyway ..."

The new chip worked like a charm, and instead of showing a name, it just registered as "user entry." It was probably unthinkable that someone would take a chip, activate it, and then use it. These chips were given out through voluntary acceptance or voluntary denial and never forced (at least that was what they said).

Nicolai left the driveway and could only think of one place to go:

black suet village three. That was where he met Tyrisha, and that was where he thought he might find some answers. He drove to the village, and it was deserted, of course. He parked his government car at the gate and went into the village, leaving that vehicle for the last time. He disliked even the commute to his meaningless job and that car was a part of all of that. He was glad to leave it behind. Nicolai looked around and then remembered Tyrisha's house number: 113. He went to the house, and the door was open. Nicolai walked inside to survey the place, feeling like an answer would appear. He had never even been so close to these mud huts.

He gathered his thoughts and then said to himself, Man, look at this place. It is of such poor construction. The kitchen is less than primitive, with poor ventilation. No one would want to live here.

Nicolai heard Leviticus's footsteps and realized he was not alone in the house. He dropped his bag and slowly walked to the next room. As he turned the corner, Leviticus tackled him to the ground.

"Who are you?" Leviticus asked roughly.

"Nicolai, my name is Nicolai."

He asked back suspiciously, "Why does that name sound familiar?"

Nicolai didn't like the way this was going, but he knew he could defend himself if need be. Nicolai gave this attacker a shift of perspective as he fought to gain dominance, and now, he had him in a headlock.

Nicolai said in a strained voice, "Listen, I don't know who you are, and I don't really care right now. Whatever you think I want to do to you, I don't, all right? I'm going to let go of you now, and I want you to calm down and realize there is no need to attack me. I'm not a threat to you."

Nicolai let go of Leviticus slowly, and they both got to their feet, glad to have not encountered a person of worse company.

"Who are you?" Leviticus asked. "Some spy sent here to further punish Derogates and those who would hide?"

Nicolai let some air out, almost laughing, and said, "No, I am someone who was a Knower and broke Knower laws and didn't like the lifestyle I was told to have. There is nothing left for me as a Knower. What I just told you is enough to get me executed, so can a great break here?"

Leviticus had been at his former house, just reminiscing. He knew it wasn't a smart idea, but he figured the Knowers would not go back to the villages to see if people were there. Moments before he heard Nicolai enter the house, he had been sitting down and crying, thinking about his mother, his wife, Zeneth, and his only treasured daughter, Tyrisha.

Nicolai still had not proven his case with words. "Look at my hand." He wiped off the makeup that covered his wound. "I took the incision out and am on the run. This is no joke or trick. I came here to see if there were any supplies left or anyone to help, for that matter."

Leviticus still did not seem convinced.

Nicolai pointed out, "Look, if I was a Knower scout, you would be dead or transported by now. Can't you see I'm alone? We both know Circle soldiers don't travel alone these days. It's too dangerous."

"Fine, I'm Leviticus, and I was just scouting around, kind of like you." Leviticus wasn't going to give this new stranger any personal information, at least not yet. "I know a place where it's safe to go. It's a three-day journey if you are up to it, but I warn you: If you have some type of tracing technology on you, they'll find it."

Leviticus didn't trust this guy, but the truth was, he was still breathing. Maybe he would just feel him out for the next couple of days; he could always ditch this Nicolai if things got weird. These days, it was safer to travel in a pair, anyway. Just take what happened to Leviticus on his way there. He managed to dodge some murdering thieves on a trail, who killed some poor soul who happened to be spotted before him. He crept around the scene, since a man could be killed for just what he had on his body. The men had weapons, and as much as Leviticus wanted to help, the odds of succeeding were very slim.

"All right, Leviticus, I understand all what you are saying, and I accept. After all, I find myself with no place to go and no one to care about what happens to me. Finding you here is the best thing that's happened to me today."

Leviticus and Nicolai headed into the forest together. They chatted and didn't have to worry about Knowers patrols. Most Knowers were more concerned with where more shipments of drugs, alcohol, and food coming in. Nicolai felt relaxed about his situation, even though he had no idea what exactly that was. The two days went by fast, and Nicolai kind of liked the traveling and quiet time he experienced. Everything had been so busy with the work, worries, bad news, strange events, and the betrayals. That stupid halovision was ruling his life. If he wasn't watching news, it was shows, movies, Wednesdays zombie church, and games taking up his time. It was peaceful out there in the wilderness; it felt like those things just didn't exist out there. Nicolai wondered why he never took time to just go outside and relax in the peace of nature. He liked this Leviticus fellow. He seemed to be a man of many words and was very likeable. He was the type of man you would go to for solid advice. He knew he was a Derogate from how he spoke, and he hoped to figure out more of what this man and his people believed in and why.

Chapter 25

Zim Jones was working at the end of the day, as usual, in his heavy dozer. He was a heavy bald guy who made jokes about being well, fat. He also made fun of other people who were fat as contradictive as that was. Food, jokes, and baseball were the life for him. He did the same thing he always did, except this time, these trenches were pretty full. At least, they were more full than usual. He picked up a bucket full of dirt and then dumped it into a trench. It was the end of the day, and as the sun was lowering toward the edge of the horizon, something strange took place. Jones felt something was out of the ordinary. He shut the dozer off, took out his earplugs, and had a confused look on his face.

"What was that?" he asked himself out loud, looking into the barren, flat lands. Goose bumps started to sprout all over his arms. He walked toward the large trench and looked in the distance toward the horizon, which the sun had dipped below. He manned up and walked toward the very edge of the trench. There, he actually took the time to look at what he was burying with his giant earth-moving machine. There, in the trench, lay thousands of bodies. These men, women, and children would not take the mark and had earned death. They were the ones who didn't make it to any prisons. The idea of prison only lasted awhile until the drought, and then everything else became scarce. The executions had been increasing in number, and those in prison who failed to acknowledge the Exalter were beheaded. More and more Derogates and even some Knowers who chose to follow those radicals raving about the Only were also beheaded. All those headless corpses lay there with heads toppled here and there.

Of course, Jones didn't focus as hard as he could because he didn't want to remember these images. Some images are easily seen but never forgotten. He was still surveying the scene and realized that the trench he had been working on was about five miles long. He thought to himself that was as much as eighty-eight football fields; this was some massive gravesite.

As he was thinking, there was nothing but silence. Then all of the sudden, with no warning, He heard something that shocked him. After hearing it, he turned and sprinted away from the trench. He fell over in his frantic retreat from something invisible. He didn't even get back into that dozer. Instead, he slow jogged his heavy frame away from there, running the half mile distance to the main base.

Jones ran into the base and reported to his superior, drenched in sweat and out of breath as he puffed all around. He hadn't run like that since high school, and the huffing showed it.

"B-b-boss, huff, huff, I'm just not," he began, pausing for to speak between breaths, "I ain't goin' back out there to that dozer. G-g-get someone else. Give me a new assignment."

His supervisor responded, "Jones, what is your problem? Did you tip the dozer over or something? Is it malfunctioning? We can get it fixed."

Jones looked down at the floor the whole time, panting as he shook his head at the questions. "No, none of that. I heard something out there. I can't explain it … and I … I ain't sayin' this ever again, so don't ask me to. The only way I can say it is this … I heard what sounded like a bunch of voices whispering, and they all said the same thing. I can't go back there. I just can't; get someone else."

Jones's supervisor looked at him with disbelief. "All right, Jones, I suppose Murphy can finish filling the trench. But tell me this, Mr. Hears Voices: What exactly did the voices say?"

Jones glanced up for the first time and looked his supervisor right in the eye. "They all said, 'Avenge us.'"

His coworkers laughed it up at Jones's expense. One even said, "I think Jones has eaten too many twinkies, Captain!" The laughing continued, but it was all too real for Jones; he didn't care how he looked; he knew what he heard.

Chapter 26

Everyone on the line was ready for action. The reports were in, and the Russians had formed an alliance of some crucial value. Dead center of Mongolia, the still faithful Circle soldiers deployed from the United States were waiting in hastily made trenches. Reports in from the Exalter had informed the men and women that a militia was forming and working to rid all people in their path. The job of the Circle soldiers was to not only defend them from advancing but to eradicate them in their tracks. The sun was still in the middle of the sky, and then there in the distance, something came into view. The militia was on its way indeed. Four tanks rode behind the militia as the soldiers walked in one large group. The Circle soldiers simply waited for the militia to get close enough; their plan was to try to work it out with communication or at least give the militia a chance to surrender. The line of militia was now thirty feet from the Circle soldiers, and no one had engaged each other. The militia leader at the front of the line held his hand up, and the militia stopped all at once.

Just then, they all heard a huge crashing thud. The Circle soldiers looked up after the dust cleared, and no one could believe it.

Tyranus had free-fallen, without a parachute, from high enough that no one even heard the aircraft. Everyone was stunned and unable to move. Tyranus was in a kneeling position as the dust cloud around him settled, and he slowly stood up to his full height. He was to the left of the militia line. He stepped out of the small crater his landing had caused; this armored beast was as wide as four average-sized men. He gazed at the row of men and women in front of him with his piercing yellow eyes.

Five soldiers stood from his left to right, and the line he saw looked like a small corn field with stalks instead of men. His armor glistened with gold and silver. His helmet was most terrifying of all. His eyes, rock-hard cheeks, nose, and facial area were slightly visible. The helmet had what looked like boomerangs facing upward on each side. The curve of the metal attachments went out and then in, like the letter V sideways. His helmet was polished and had sharp points on each side where his jaw bone almost met his face. The helmet made him look like a powerful alien being. Tyranus simply walked slowly out of the crater.

A Circle general looked with wide eyes and said, "Where from hell did that thing come from?"

The militia soldiers turned to face Tyranus and raised their weapons. After all, this was the first time that anyone had seen a super soldier, and it was absolutely an amazing entrance. The soldiers fired their weapons, but they had no effect. As they fired, Tyranus sprinted at the soldiers with his arms spread out like an eagle soaring in the wind; as he ran, he trampled the soldiers and knocked them all down with such force that most of them were killed. After he ran through the soldiers, he looked around and turned toward the militia's tanks.

One of the tanks began firing the turret gun at Tyranus' chest, but the bullets just bounced off like dead flies. Tyranus flipped it over five times with one mighty stroke of his right arm. The other tanks fired rounds at Tyranus, but he literally crushed one tank into scrap with repeated downward blows. The second tank he seemed bent on chopping up. He struck it with chopping motions down the middle, with both of his hands set in a praying motion. The third and fourth tanks fired at him, but the blasts simply didn't faze him. Tyranus lifted up one tank and used it to smash the other tank to bits. After he was done, he took the tank above his head and threw it an impressive distance grunting loudly as he did so. He walked slowly back to the line of Circle soldiers.

The super soldier faced them and raised his right hand to the sky. "I am Tyranus; fear me, for I am powerfully made. Hail the Exalter, who is creator of all." His voice was so with deep bass and loud, it carried great lengths. He then lowered his hand and said, "Death to all who oppose him."

Just then, a helicopter appeared and hovered above him; Tyranus simply bent his knees and leaped forty feet into the air, jumping into the chopper. The fear that engulfed the hearts of the Circle soldiers was obvious. The rumors and worship mixed with fear had given the Exalter what he wanted: submission by fear.

Chapter 27

"Of course I heard the trumpets, you idiot," the Exalter snapped. "Do you think he wouldn't have opened my ears to it?" The Exalter was in a furious state inside, while trying to show control on the outside.

The Seer replied, "Well, I was just curious, my lord. I heard it myself, as well. I know he thinks he can use music to mock you. He would do that considering your beginning."

The Exalter responded, "Candon, you are my most trusted subject, but your comment brings up enough memories for me to kill you and ruin your family for generations. I made the worship music here on earth a wonderful sound, and I am able to change the ending of the story. Do you think I cannot?"

The Seer realized that his comment was not well thought out. Trying to placate the Exalter, he said, "Of course you can, my lord. You can do anything that is possible and even perform the impossible."

The Exalter gave him a murderous glare and left the room, walking down the hall to the waiting podium, where he began his speech:

"Good evening, my loyal subjects. Some of you may be wondering what happened today in the eastern attacks in Mongolia. I have introduced a loyal subject of mine, and you all have seen him with your own eyes. I don't need to appear in such a form as to intimidate any of you. In fact, if I showed my real form to you, my presence would overwhelm you. I will remain as I am until the day you breathe your last breath, and then, I will meet you in paradise. However, the point of me talking to you now is to remind you that you are either with me or against me. Those who are against me will suffer the consequences of breaking my laws. They will face death; I will send them to the eternal pit of fire, where they will suffer for eternity. Test me in this and see if my voice doesn't prove to be true.

"Today in Mongolia, I unleashed Tyranus. You in the United States will be seeing my other powerful servant, Granite, and those of you in the West will see Jupiter. These three powerful subjects are a force larger than any of you have ever seen. Through them, those of you who would doubt me will see that my power is unlimited, and anyone who tries to get in the way will face a swift death. Now, there is no need for anyone to fear. I never said there wouldn't be tests and trials, as they make you stronger. I have given you the choice of life or death, so choose to live. It is not hard; all you have to do is serve me and follow the decisions that I make for you. I know the right direction for you. I created you, and I love you. I realize that many of these rebellions and false followers have created major problems for this planet, trying to poison our supply lines, creating diseases, and more recently, working to try to change the climate of this planet. I'm not a creator that would control you and therefore I have not and will not take away free will.

"We must work together to form a new alliance and replace the Derogates with those who will pledge their allegiance to me. Be patient. Supplies, food, and provisions are on their way to you. I would not lie to you, I cannot, and I will never let you down. I love everything that I have created. Continue on, and your rewards from me will overflow your households."

With that, the feed to the Exalter shut off. Some people bought it like a Sunday sale. Others heard what was said and waited for the end result with hope. The third group didn't buy any of it; they thought, If this guy was really the creator of the universe, then why didn't he eradicate diseases, kill all who oppose him, and make it rain?

Chapter 28

The super soldier Granite made his first appearance off of a large ship pulling into the Baltimore harbor. The militia attacks continued, even after Tyranus's display of power. Some people still wanted to take down these monsters, as if they were breaking a Guinness world record. Granite's armor was navy blue and silver, with black also mixed in. His helmet was different from Tyranus's. Granite's black helmet fit his head perfectly to the skin; all you could see were those strange, piercing blue eyes. All three of the supermen had eyes that almost glowed when they looked at you, like flashlights in the dark. A royal blue metal piece covered his nose and face. Three solid black vertical lines were spaced out on the nose and face piece. The strange design was mysterious and fearful. Granite patrolled the harbor as two precious items were arriving: flour and salt. He simply paced the harbor back and forth; many people figured it would be a fitting place to fight anyway. Fort McHenry was in plain view, so why not give it another whirl? Of course, that is exactly what Granite wanted to happen.

Granite flew backward more than fifty feet. What on earth could have moved a monster like that? A rebel jet had fired a missile right at Granite, and it had clipped his right shoulder. When the smoke cleared, many of the Circle soldiers looked at Granite, and their helmet camera feed would later be displayed on the news report to strengthen confidence in the Exalter. Granite stood up slowly to survey his area. Everyone was just amazed. This guy had just been hit by a missile but was still standing.

The super soldier climbed to the top of his vessel and strapped on some type of backpack. This was no ordinary backpack. After he put on the large pack, Granite tapped a button and two wings shot out from the bottom of the pack powered by cell boosters. In an instant, he was airborne and quickly flew above the rebel jet pilot. He timed it perfectly and landed right on top of the jet. Granite punched a hole in the middle of the jet and then smashed one of the wings. He then smashed the other wing, and the jet began to nosedive. The pilot was sweating and knew at this altitude, the only option was to eject.

He hit the button, and the top came off, as Granite was waiting for the pilot to make a move. The pilot flew past Granite and detached from his seat as his parachute opened. Granite leaped off the jet and soared up to the rebel pilot, who was now descending. He grabbed the man with his huge bear paws for hands, and they both fell at an accelerated rate of speed (the parachute wasn't much use with the extra weight). They both hit the water, and people waited to see who would emerge.

It was Granite; he came out of the water and climbed up a ship in the harbor with his prisoner, leaping massive distances from ship to ship until he was on the harbor wall. Once at the wall, Granite set the pilot down and raised his right hand; he made a fist, and a long sharp blade emerged from the end of his arm. In one swoop, the pilot was beheaded, right there in front of everyone: passersby, military, and oh, yes, the entire world watching on live halovision. Many teenagers jeered the act on desensitized by now from all the public beheadings.

So far, the super soldiers had taken down tanks and jets. What else did the rebels have in their collection to combat these one-man armies?

That same day, a large convoy of flatbed trucks were driving through the Midwest. A cloud of dust trailed behind all the trucks as they continued on. Two Hummers with men on turrets also traveled with this group, in order to protect the precious supplies. The rebels were not far off. This time, an indirect attack seemed to be best. A team of four snipers sat on the north cliffs; the sun beat down on everything in the dusty land. Each sniper was aiming at a different semitrailer, intending to take out the driver of each truck. Then, the men on the turrets and anyone else could be picked off easily, if the plan went well that is.

In a distance, the rebel militia were waiting for the radio signal once the snipers cleared the area. However, Jupiter was bent on keeping the convoy safe. One of the snipers noticed something rather strange. He followed the perplexing sight with his sniper scope. That was no dust devil. Something was spewing up dust as it sped through the land. There was nothing to be seen except the dust, but whatever it was, it was coming close.

Jupiter had been riding next to the convoy on his oversized motorcycle. Of course, no one could see him, as his motorcycle was cloaked by secret technology. As he rode with the convoy, he was completely undetected, even by the drivers. Jupiter had looked toward the cliffs to the north and heat signatures from the waiting snipers.

One sniper said quickly, "Hey, guys, something is approaching us fast at eleven o'clock."

The snipers all looked, but it was too late. The thing approaching them was upon them, and as the dust trail came closer, Jupiter uncloaked himself and became visible, appearing out of thin air. He calmly slid his motorcycle sideways, and it came to a stop. He reached for the scepter on his back. As he pulled that scepter high, the eyes of all the snipers went right to it. The size of this weapon was astonishing. One side of the scepter was a half-moon-shaped blade, and the other side was a hard, metal hammer. Between the hammer and the blade was a solid red circle.

Jupiter's black armor was also unique. Between the seams, his armor was red and orange. None of his skin was exposed, and his armor had all types of detection technology. With his helmet, his eyes could zoom in at will, detect heat signatures, use night vision, and even examine an opposing soldier's vital signs, using x-ray technology. His vision could even pierce through thick walls. The top of his reddish orange helmet looked just like a hammer head shark. His eyes were covered by a solid silver shield that could not be seen through from the outside. This instilled fear into the five snipers' hearts, as what you can't see is often what scares you the most. The men could taste the adrenaline in their mouths.

The militia opened fire with their sidearms and even threw grenades, but Jupiter simply walked toward them; these tough snipers were now scared little puppies. Jupiter approached the first sniper, who opened fire with his large-caliber rifle, but the super soldier was not even stunned. Jupiter made one quick swoop, and the sniper's head fell to the ground. The other three men were all smashed with the heavy hammer end of his scepter. The last sniper was kept alive, as Jupiter left a witness behind to communicate what had happened.

Jupiter clutched the sniper's chest, and a device came out of Jupiter's armor and grabbed the man's communication device. One could only guess that Jupiter's massive hand was too big to operate such a device without destroying it. He simply pressed the button for the transmission, as Jupiter wanted to trace where signal was going. Through his chrome visor, he could see exactly where the signal went. He watched as the blue-white jagged electric line ran through the air, pinpointing the location of where the transmission went.

Jupiter turned his back on the sniper and continued to his motorcycle. Just as he smashed and destroyed the snipers, he did the same to the other rebel militia, using special grenades that killed all organic matter. The blast radius could be seen from above, where there was a circle of dead trees and plant life. Once again, Jupiter had thrown one of the militia members outside the blast area so that he would be a lone survivor.

Jupiter would have rather killed all the men and gloated over his awesome power. However, these strong brutes were still controlled by the Exalter. And the Exalter wanted witnesses in order to discourage more attacks. It is one thing to observe an attack and ponder how to change your tactics in response. It is another thing to talk with a survivor who can describe things in great detail, planting fear and making strong men's hearts go weak.

Chapter 29

"Where is he hiding? I want you to find him."

Kiyana was infuriated that Nicolai was playing these games. She was ready for him to face his judgment for his treason and breaking the holy Exalter's laws, and for trying to blackmail Cedro. In the past, her heart may have loved Nicolai, and even now, she thought she loved Nicolai more than Cedro if she was real with herself. However, her actions were not so convincing. It is a strange thing how people can give their absolute devotion to one person, and then, in time, like an old car, they don't see its value anymore.

The former Knower soldier, now a Circle soldier, said impatiently, "The signal is coming from upstairs."

The man continued walking with Kiyana, who knew he had orders to take Nicolai in. Janae was in the background as a spectator, just watching the manhunt unfold in front of her eyes.

The Circle soldier and Kiyana entered Nicolai's bedroom (it was really only his bedroom; they had stopped sleeping in the same room long ago).

Janae walked into the room and stood in front of the window. The soldier used his scanning device and stopped at Nicolai's nightstand.

"What the? I don't think he's in that drawer," the soldier said sarcastically.

Kiyana reached for the only picture on the nightstand. The chip was exactly where Nicolai had left it, in order to send a silent message to Kiyana.

"It's here," Kiyana said, sounding puzzled and frustrated.

She held the photo close to see what the commotion was, and upon viewing the photo, she traveled back in time with her memories. The picture showed a beautiful young couple in their fancy white marriage garments, and the perfect sunset in the background. The picture was Nicolai's favorite picture and Kiyana knew that.

Kiyana teleported back into that moment in time.

The wedding photographer had said, "All right, folks, that is the last one. Congratulations, and I will have these over to you by the evening."

Nicolai turned and gave Kiyana a passionate stare, as he looked deep into those blue eyes.

"Kiyana," he vowed, "I am going to make you so happy. I promise to always be faithful to you and give you my unbreakable devotion. I will never leave you … ever."

It was one of those moments when the world stops; Kiyana looked into Nicolai's blue eyes and responded, "I am already so happy. You make me feel like my life has a great purpose. I won't ever leave you either my love, and you have all the faithfulness my heart can give."

Kiyana's eyes started to tear up as the past memory was too hard to face and made her numb heart start to feel again. Then her eyes shifted to the chip that was placed behind the picture frame, and she became enraged. She unfolded a white piece of paper. It was a Triune document for divorce, with Nicolai's signature on the bottom and a blank space waiting for hers. She thought about how Nicolai had left her and realized that she had left first; this was Nicolai's way of saying, "You left me a long time ago. See, I can leave too."

Kiyana wouldn't let herself be the one in the wrong, even if she had to lie to herself. She threw the frame against the wall, and the glass shattered.

She yelled, "Find him! Find him and make him pay."

$\mathcal{C}$hapter 30

Leviticus and Nicolai were only one day away from the waterfall compound, where they would be safe. They had reached that point where each person drops his defensive shield and is ready to spill out his life story. They continued to chat as Leviticus led the way down uncharted trails. Nicolai was telling him about Kiyana and how he broke into Cedro's house.

He began to describe how there was a hidden cell and how he remembered the number 252 on those abandoned clothes. Leviticus stopped walking abruptly, his eyes widened, and he began to feel his heart thumping in his chest.

"Did you say number 252?"

Nicolai replied, "Yeah, why?"

Leviticus's voice began to rise and he said, "Tell me what else you saw. Was she there? Did you see her?"

Nicolai replied, "Huh, she? Who? I don't know about that, but I do know one thing. There was nothing, just the clothes and shoes in an empty room; it looked like a secret holding chamber."

Leviticus was trying to contain his thoughts. "Wait a minute," he said. "This other Knower. Did he have a tattoo of a lion on the left side of his neck? Was his name Cedro?"

The obvious answer came back, "Yeah, that's right."

Leviticus began walking in the direction they had come from.

"Leviticus? Where are you going?"

"I am going to kill Cedro. He is a dead man. That number 252 was my mother, and I bet he kept her there for his own sick reasons. She always said that he made passes at her in front of my father. I will give him what he deserves, and I don't care what happens to me."

Nicolai took in what was said and thought it out. "No, no, wait a minute. Cedro didn't even know about your mother or the secret cell. He told me that Xyla, his partner, had the cell built and put her in there."

"Yeah, right; what makes you think he would tell you the truth? He is a snake."

"I know he told me the truth because I had him tied up, and he knew his life was in jeopardy; I forced the truth out of him. Plus, the schematics weren't in the design for the building. Someone did it secretly. If Cedro wanted June bad enough, he could have brought her into his house as one of his own wives. Don't you see it? Xyla had it done in order to get your mom out of the way because she felt threatened by her or whatever. If you go now, you are a dead man. Think about it ..."

Leviticus took a deep breath, closed his eyes, and exhaled as he stared straight up into the sky. "You said her clothes were there and her shoes?"

Nicolai replied, "Yes."

Leviticus said, speaking calmly now, "Then there is hope. My mother was taken in the great disappearance by the Only. She and my father must be reunited in heaven, where they have found happiness that no one can take from them. However, Xyla must pay for what she did to my family."

Nicolai was willing to go on a little faith, but there was no solid belief on his part. He then asked, "Do you think this Only that your people believe in will make Xyla pay?"

Leviticus said, "Oh, I know he will make her pay. He says it in his book that the evil will perish. He will be my vindicator. But I still wish my hand was in on it."

They continued their trip to the secret waterfall compound; Nicolai was ready to find a new home.

Chapter 31

Candon Veswalis, also known as the Seer, was talking patiently with his master.

"My lord, you have demonstrated your power with your super soldiers. However, the deniers are still numerous, the militia continues to up rise, and the earth's condition is predictably unstable. I am sure that you know all this. However, I think now that you have shown the power of your force, it is time to demonstrate your provision to a world in need, so they may once again serve you wholeheartedly."

The Exalter stood and looked out the window at the early evening twilight. He began, "I have been on this earth a very long time, feeling trapped by its borders. It is only fitting that I should rule it forever. I should be the one with the greatest reward and the one with the most power. I have shown my power, but now it is time for them to believe in my miracles."

The next day, a conference was held in San Francisco.

"Is everything as I asked it to be, Candon?" the Exalter asked.

"Yes, my lord, it all has been placed as you wish."

"Very good, then."

The Exalter walked across the stage and stood at the podium. The people all bowed in allegiance to him.

Earlier that morning, a young man named Fuero had been experiencing troubles, including hearing voices in his head. This had never happened before. Was he going crazy? Those same voices drove him to find his father's old pistol and load it. The voices rang out continuously, and he couldn't take it anymore. The young man could find no rest. He grabbed a hoody jacket and left for the conference. There was only one thing to do to get the voices to stop, and that was to do what they were commanding.

The Exalter stared across the sea of people who were there to simply see him; others were waiting for answers, and others yet expected provisions from their leader.

Was no one watching? Where was security? The man in the hoodie walked out of nowhere and headed quickly toward the Exalter, who did not even turn to acknowledge him. By this time, his handgun was pointed directly at the Exalter's head. The voices in Fuero's head were getting angrier as they commanded him. Everyone else had frozen; they were scared the Exalter would be hurt, but why? Wasn't he god?

Fuero wasted no time and squeezed the trigger, hoping to end the agony of the voices that repeated, "Kill the Exalter. Kill him ... You have to kill him, or we will never leave. Go kill him. Do it. Do it now! Do it!" Over and over, the voices ranted on, and the recoil of the gun going off in Fuero's hand ended the struggle.

The Exalter's head cocked to the right from the impact, as brain matter spread out from the barrel's edge, but he didn't go down. He was still standing. The Exalter's head tilted slowly from the cockeyed position and straightened back up. The wounds were healing right in full view of the people present and all those watching on the global network.

He turned to Fuero slowly and smiled, "My son, I understand your frustration, and I forgive you for what you tried to accomplish. Do not fear, for I am the start and the finish, and I will give you all you seek." He turned to the men in suits standing nearby and added, "Take this man away and give him supplies and provisions so he may return home to his family."

Fuero tried to speak out quickly before the Terafin guards came to hustle him along. Only the few who were close heard Fuero ranting,

"Wait a minute. It wasn't me! I didn't do that. They made me do it. They made me do it."

The global network didn't show any of this, naturally. The Exalter looked over the crowd, as everyone was just in complete awe. If this man in the flesh could show such godly miracles, he had to be who he said he was, right?

He began his speech, which had everyone's attention eye popping attention at this point.

"There has been a drought that you all are very aware of. There are things in life that are a test. That young man came to test me. He came to see if I would fall and die and prove to be a liar. You see today that I am not. You see today that I am who I say I am. I simply am … Tests will come in your lives, and those tests will mold you into stronger human beings. Behold, I have given you a test; many of you have passed, and for the righteousness of those tests, I will provide. I will not let one righteous family suffer because of those who deny me. My desire is for all to know me, and I am saddened for those who will not come to me. Let my tears blanket this earth and, in doing so, also heal the ground."

The Exalter closed his eyes and looked down, with the Pacific Ocean behind him as the backdrop. He slowly raised both of his hands in the air. In the distance, a mist started to form quickly between the ocean and the clouds. Then within a minute, clouds began to form in the air and moved right over the people.

The Exalter gave out his last sentence: "Now honor me, pray to me, and see if I do not shower you with the gifts of heaven until your houses overflow."

He walked away from the podium, and no one even noticed because it started raining. It had not rained for so long. The people just enjoyed being showered with the rain. A large wall of rain started from that point and ran an entire circle around the globe until every country had been blessed by this precipitation. The miracle of healing and now needed rain seemed to be the pivotal paramount of the Exalter's miracles.

Chapter 32

A fancy package was sitting on the doorstep of Cedro's house. He was feeling better than ever, knowing that Nicolai was out of the picture. He was equally thrilled that his undercover business was doing very well, as the sale of alcohol and drugs continued to boom. Good thing he had warehouses filled with this stuff. Cedro had returned from a jog late that morning when he noticed the package; he brought it inside and unwrapped it, filled with curiosity. Inside the package were bottles of different alcoholic drinks, and in the middle of it all was one red apple, which seemed very out of place.

Cedro thought, *What is that red apple all about?*

He unfolded the card in his hands and read, "You and your household are invited to the headquarters of the Exalter tomorrow evening at the Triune, to attend a small party for honored Knower guests."

This was great, Cedro thought; now he knew he was the man, with the approval of the Exalter. That night, he shared the alcohol with Xyla and his other two body partner wives.

Before they all knew it, the next day had come, and they drove up to the Triune feeling pretty groggy.

The massive stone building was impressive, with sculptures of animals on the pillars, and other accents, which they noticed as their eyes scanned the area. Cedro, Xyla, and his other two wives were dressed at their best. Their robot guardians also traveled with them and followed behind them.

A man greeted them at the door, took the signature key, and parked their vehicle for them. They were escorted into the building by other servants.

They were guided to a table that was covered by a fancy white tablecloth, with nothing else on it. Five chairs were arranged around the circular table, and the four of them sat down, expecting to be served with other guests. However, there was no one else in the room. There was no one around. A great door opened that stood the length of the ceiling.

The Exalter's Terafin guards opened the doors and stood in front of them. There was no mistaking those distinguished red capes that draped each shoulder, the scepters they carried, or the armor that enveloped them. Cedro and his wives' smiles and laughter began to fade somewhat as they looked to see what would happen next. Their robot protectors were usually right behind them, no matter what they did in public, but now, they had stayed along the wall, fading into the shadows and powering down.

As expected, the Exalter walked through the doors and began walking right toward them. Cedro and his wives went to one knee in honor of the Exalter and bowed their heads low. They had gone from happy to fearful in a second. Especially Cedro, as he had so much to hide and worry about. The Exalter took a seat in the fifth chair as a servant brought him a crystal glass filled with sparkling clear water. Two other servants brought a plate and arranged the other dinnerware and utensils just so.

The Exalter took a drink of the water and said afterward, "Do any of you know my real name?" He looked around for a second and continued, "I didn't think so. My earthly name here is Laykeun Rapportyne. I tell you that because I feel it is important to know things about each other that we don't know. Cedro, do you have anything you want to tell me?"

Cedro's cowardly fear prompted him to consider falling apart and bursting into tears. This overconfident, pig-headed womanizer was experiencing real fear for the first time. The feeling was not setting well. What did the Exalter mean? What did he know?

Cedro swallowed and began, "My lord, you know my household serves you and that we are faithful to you. You are … our god."

The Exalter showed no sign of approval or disapproval of Cedro's words. He was completely unreadable. "Cedro, if I know everything as you say, then I ought to show you such." The Exalter looked at one of his guards. "Bring him in."

A man in ragged clothes was tossed in the room; he appeared frightened almost to death. Did they pull this guy out of a condemned dungeon or what? He looked awful.

The Exalter commanded, "Tell them what you told me."

The Derogate's faded clothes still identified him as number 387; he sobbed, looking downward, and said, "They were going to kill me because I wouldn't take the incision. I told them I had information about one of their own defying their Exalter. They didn't believe me, so I gathered my materials and showed them what I knew. I told them how I had been making drugs and how I had been ordered to have Derogates forge incorrect numbers on shipments for other Derogates who were working for Knowers."

The Exalter interrupted, "That is some story, Mr. 387, thank you. Please take him away to the gallows and kill him quite quickly. Oh, how the deifiers bother me so." The Exalter exhaled a sigh of relief to know that awful Derogate would be killed. Then he made eye contact with Cedro as he made a charming smile showing no teeth.

A Circle soldier appeared out of the shadows and dragged the Derogate away as the man yelled and screamed in the background with predictable pleas for his life.

Cedro and his wives knew exactly where this was going. They were all stuck; each moment could be their last dying breath. The feeling could be compared to being tied down on train tracks and watching a locomotive in the distance, coming at you, while you knew exactly how it ended: with your life.

The Exalter continued as a meal was coming in the room for him already, "Well, he tells of mysteries of false believers who think they can rob God. We have one filthy Derogate who at least tells the truth and has unraveled an interesting tale of four mysteries. Mystery one, who gave him all these drugs stolen from my shipments? Mystery two, who thought up this scheme to forge shipments? Mystery three, who provided payments of drugs and alcohol to those involved? And finally, mystery four, who has what he thought was three secret accounts with more than two trillion Aeons in each of them? I might add, who is also paying all three of his housewives to keep silent? He recently gave an increased payment to one in particular."

Cedro closed his eyes in agony, looked down, and let out a deep breath as his face flushed.

Xyla chimed in, "My lord, you must know I have been keeping all of this on record and came to you with this news so that your will could be performed."

Cedro's head shot back as he turned to give Xyla a "I can't believe you" look. The other two wives also started to beg for their lives.

What could Cedro say? He was caught so deep, there was no digging out now. The Terafins must have sensed the rise in emotions as they came forward and slammed their scepters on the floor, standing on each side of the Exalter. The thuds brought all the female voices to a stop. A servant brought out the Exalter's entrée, and he began eating completely unmoved.

After chewing, he spoke again, still surprisingly calm as his company was waiting on the edge of his words: "I know all of you are sorry. I really do. However, those who say they are my children and yet defy me will not see the kingdom of my domain. Instead, they will see what you see, and that is a bucket waiting for your heads to fall in, and then the inescapable fire. Take them all to be executed for their blasphemy, except this one. Leave her here."

Left at the table was the one and only Xyla. Cedro began acting like a complete coward, sobbing and crying. His other two wives were taking the news better, as they simply murmured in tears, knowing they were facing death, the thing most feared by many. They yelled at Cedro that their deaths were all his fault. It was sad they were going to die but even more perplexing that they couldn't take responsibility for their own actions, making Cedro the scapegoat.

The Exalter motioned for a plate for Xyla. She spoke quickly as usual, trying to steer the conversation her way. "My lord, I am loyal to only you, and I am ready to do whatever you need me to do for you. I can do anything you ask and even more."

The Exalter changed from his unreadable tone to one that was much more real. "Xyla serves ... only Xyla," he began. "Enough with your lies. The only reason you are still alive is because I know you will be loyal to yourself by keeping yourself alive. I have seen many generations of your kind taking men for everything they have, even to the point where men take their own lives because of it. Its strange but I admire how you try to be the lord of your own life. Of course, I can identify with that. No, you are only alive because I am giving you one more chance with my forgiveness. You don't even deserve my forgiveness for what you have done, but I will use you as you have used men. You will locate this secret lair of the false believers and rebels that I have heard of. Perhaps there is even more than one location. That is up to you to find out. I will require detailed knowledge of schematics, plans, and any other information that my security forces may find useful. You report only to me. Talk to anyone about this, and you are as good as your headmaster, who might have two parts to him out back by now. What is your answer?"

Xyla liked the idea for a new start serving the much famed Exalter. She was on the top of the world, in her eyes. She didn't even feel the loss of her three family members, who were most likely gone by now. "You know, I will do it, my lord."

She smiled and then took a bite of the plate that was brought out for her.

"Yes, I knew you would, Xyla. You will make a small trip to one of my dentists after you are done here. But first that incision must come out. If you think this is a free token to escape, you will realize you can do nothing without it. Now, consider this a small form of punishment for what you have done."

One of the Terafin guards walked closer as Xyla edged away in her seat, showing her fear for the first time at the visit. The Terafin grabbed her right hand, exposed a knife, and removed the incision in a less-than-gentle manner. Her screams could be heard from the hall outside the banquet doors. At least she still had her life. Only minutes ago, Cedro and his other two wives heard the last sound of the angled blade coming down on their necks. As they all considered their lives, they had come to the same conclusion: Their lives had meant nothing. No real accomplishments, and nothing that made the world a better place—only greed. They were all thinking they had more to time to amount to something purposeful. They all wanted a second chance they would never be afforded.

Chapter 33

Leviticus and Nicolai were at last in sight of the waterfall. Leviticus led the way, and they made it to the waterfall and went behind the large stream, just as Leviticus had done before. They went through the same secret doors and infrared lighting and drying systems, and then the large doors closed behind them. Next, they went through the scanners. Leviticus walked through with no problem. After Nicolai went through, the guards started to encircle him.

Leviticus spoke up, "Hey, guys, what's the problem?"

One guard spoke loudly and said with authority, "Step back, sir."

Just then, four walls started to come out of the floor. They rose up and surrounded them in a small space. Then from above, a black horizontal slab descended formed an enclosed ceiling. Inside, the guards had their weapons drawn on Nicolai, who naturally stretched out his hands in innocence.

As two guards kept their weapons on Nicolai, another one moved in and took his right hand; he asked, "Where's the chip?"

"I took it out of my hand," he explained.

The guard was not satisfied with that answer. "I said, where is the chip?"

Nicolai just put it together. How could he forget? "Oh man, I'm sorry. I have a special chip that isn't programmed. It is just a blank chip. When the computer goes to check the signature of the chip to identify the person, it can't pinpoint that person and just chooses a previous identity as well."

The guards finished going through Nicolai's backpack, and some other questions had risen for sure. The walls came down, and Leviticus was somewhat in shock.

"Guards, where you taking him?" he asked. "What did he do?"

As the guards escorted Nicolai out, one of them responded, "This man has brought in questionable materials with him, and we have to interrogate him. Step aside, sir."

They took him down an elevator and led him to an interrogation room.

Chapter 34

Nicolai entered the room and sat down on a chair; someone was already waiting for him.

"Hi there, my name is Talique," the young man said, "and generations before me, my family built this facility. You were brought here because you have some materials that are questionable. I have been informed that you had a miracle chip that gains access into the Knower society. You also brought a surge displacer and other technology. I believe everyone deserves the right to fully explain himself, and I don't mean to be impolite, as I am respectful to everyone I meet. Just as I would want them to be with me. So please, explain yourself."

Nicolai knew he had been caught by Knowers and said, "My name is Nicolai Turner, and I have the miracle chip, as you call it, because I cut the incision out of my hand. I was to be turned in to the military for all types of crimes against the Exalter. It is all a big misunderstanding, but most is true, as I am not persuaded by the Exalter. I took the chip because I didn't know where I was going to go. I worked in an area where I learned much more than anybody ever thought I would. Processors control everything for people these days, and I found ways to change programming and other things. I have this chip in case I had to go through checkpoints or steal a vehicle. As for the surge displacer,

I had it for obvious protection. I am sure I was supposed to be buried in one of those grave trenches by now. The other equipment, I just debugged it so it wasn't traceable and was going to use it however I saw fit. Listen, I am out of options. If I go back, I am dead. I've told you the truth, so do to me what you think is right."

Talique sat back, put his hands together, looked up as if in deep thought, and responded, "Nicolai, if I put this chip right here on my right hand, would I be able to access all these points, vehicles, and manned checkpoints, without any problems?"

Nicolai let out a deep breath of air. "Yes, you could, but there is also a chance that the error on the system could make the Circle soldiers give you a manual DNA wave test right there and then. Then—boom!— you're done after ten seconds. If they don't buy a scan where they get a message showing no user name its game over again. Not to mention if they find out you have this manipulated chip, boom! You're done again."

Talique pressed his lips together and nodded to show that he got it and was thinking about it. "I'll tell you what," he said. "So far, your story is interesting. I think we need to talk more; a man with your knowledge could be very valued here. There is also a chance that you are a spy. I suppose only time will tell; in this world, on the bad side, a person's word is worthless. However, for the time being your weapon, this miracle chip and the other electronics will be confiscated. You may go upstairs and begin the introductory process, and then after you are comfortable here, we will talk again."

Talique got up and walked around to Nicolai. He put his hand on the right shoulder of Nicolai and said, "I hope and pray you have made the right decision for you and all of us."

Then Talique exited the room. On his way out, he quietly told his captain, "Put two tails on him. I want him watched."

The guards started to escort Nicolai to the elevator. He was still not easily intimidated after everything and just spat out, "So hey, guys, what was with the wall trick back there, anyway? Pretty cool stuff."

One of the soldiers said, "It wasn't you we were worried about. It was any type of signals you could have been transmitting. Most people who come here are Derogates, and those who have had the incision are to be treated as suspects until proven otherwise for the safety of the rest of the people here."

Leviticus was waiting at a table, and when he saw Nicolai, he knew everything must have been all right. Nicolai noticed him and then heard the introductions from the speakers at the entrance: "New Derogates, former Knowers, and those of you who held no allegiance, forget the past ..."

Nicolai explained it all to Leviticus, and he listened.

Even though these men had been together for days, they had not talked about the one person they had in common: Leviticus's daughter, Tyrisha. When Nicolai entered the house numbered 113, he didn't think anything of Leviticus being there, other than he was seeking shelter or looting. Leviticus hadn't been wearing his normal Derogate clothes.

They both went to a table to sit down and mentally rest, knowing their voyage from the black suet village camp was over. As they shared a cup of freeze-dried hot cocoa, they felt safe, comfortable, and relaxed. Outside the thick walls of earth, the world was dangerous, stressed, and on edge. A comparison would be the historic time where all those slaved people from the twenty first century lived. Everyone always joked about how the past civilization worked ridiculous long hours, had to actually pay for bad insurance, lived check to check, and worse they had to work for that money.

$\mathcal{C}$hapter 35

A large group of people were listening to a young woman speak about the judgments that were taking place. Who was this woman anyway? If she had so much knowledge about the Only, then why was she still here? All the deserters and past Derogates listened intently as this striking woman's voice spoke with such authority.

She continued, "Do you think the conquests of this evil government are a coincidence? They want all of us to have the incision and to submit to the will of the Exalter. He is not the Only. For if he were the Only, he would know we are here right now and appear to us. He claims to be ever powerful, so why is he allowing all of this to happen? The book that reveals all this says there has been a spirit of conquering, there has been famine and plagues, and animal attacks have been reported by both sides. They have tried to get rid of the Only and keep it a secret. This holy book has been outlawed, as he tried to set up the false kingdom against the Only. Many of you have arrived here even today, and yet you still do not know who the Exalter really is. There is a fight between good and evil, and he is evil. He is the archenemy of the true Only and his son, the archenemy of all of us, and he is the reason we are hiding in this cave right now.

"But we have all been given a second chance to repent for breaking the Only's laws. We have been in ignorance because of what the system out there has given us. Now, we have a choice for life or death. What will you choose? What will you pick when they give you the choice between having your head cut off or taking the incision? Then and only then will you know where you will be after this life and these troubled times are over. Father, I ask for your guidance for all these people. I ask for the forgiveness that we all need, as we have forsaken you and not wanted to believe. I believe that your son died on a cross for the sin of men and also believe that the world out there has worked so hard to get our eyes off of that and to hide the truth from us. Father, guide us in these hard times, amen."

The young woman stepped down; some of these people had never even heard a prayer to the Only. They only knew him as the false god. Some didn't even want to believe in either.

A young woman approached the speaker as she stepped down and said, "Tyrisha, you have done some real good here today and said what is right in these troubled times, when we are all looking for him to save us."

Shay Lyn was a twenty-two-year-old Japanese American woman. She had straight black hair and dark eyes that were very kind spirited; she was a kind-hearted person. She was someone who had it very rough from all the present circumstances, but the cheery spirited roots of her personality were still attached.

Tyrisha thanked her, and they walked together toward the inner cave.

Tyrisha had begun southeast, just as the angel had commanded. On her journey, she found Shay Lyn washing clothes in a river. After realizing that neither one was a threat, the two bonded and formed a close friendship. Shay Lyn was a Derogate from a remote village, where her tasks were very different from house cleaning. Her village's main priority was farming. Even with the sophisticated equipment, the Knowers liked to see the Derogates work extremely hard, as these orders were directly from the Exalter. Human yokes were made, and then Derogates were fastened with them as they used their force to plow a field. At least one time, Shay Lyn had helped with this slavish activity and described how dirty, exhausting, and humiliating it was. Knowers even had yokes built where five humans had to strap on the giant yoke and move the plow.

Tyrisha and Shay Lyn had exchanged stories as they both traveled. When you are a Derogate, you know what to eat in the wilderness and how to survive. When you are practically governed into close starvation, you look somewhere else than the government for provision. These two were a funny pair. One knew how to clean houses and fix small appliances, and the other was more of an expert on small game hunting, farming, growing, and harvesting. It was too bad that Tyrisha hadn't been given an occupation that helped in her current circumstances.

Shay Lyn continued her conversation in the cave, where the light poured in during the day. "You know, I am really glad that I have met you, Tyrisha. I didn't know anything about the Only, and I can see now even from that printed book we got from village eighteen that there is hope."

The pair had managed to find a partial copy of a book hidden in an area used for the village's toilet system. Everyone knew that no Knower would search that area, and they went on a hunch and were fortunate enough to find it.

"My family always believed that gaining wisdom and finding inner peace was what we should all strive for. It never really seemed to sit well with me, and I find myself truly enlightened now," Shay Lyn said.

Tyrisha was in deep thought. "I am so glad that the Only has used me to help you, Shay Lyn. I have never had a friend who also shared such a bond with me. My only other desire on this earth is to find my father before all of this is over and see my mother again in heaven, where she is waiting for me. But I guess I just have to take it one day at a time."

Shay Lyn was ready to be that friend and step in with an encouraging word, but her words were interrupted by a couple of thuds on the ground.

An explosion and a blinding light followed. Suddenly, people found themselves on the ground. Tyrisha covered her ears, which were ringing from the multiple blasts that had surrounded them. Her head hurt inside, and she felt disoriented. The Circle soldiers had thrown concussion grenades into the cave and began removing the deserters.

How had the soldiers found them? The answer was very simple: technology. A Knower named Servantés had found his way into the woods and then this cave. He left the Knower world because he felt it was the right thing to do. He felt everything was going out of control and that hiding might save him from all the violence and sicknesses. However, in doing so, he didn't realize that a single chip located under the tissue in his right hand would be picked up by military aircraft travelling the distant countryside, picking up signals.

The soldiers did pick up that signal, and now, all these people were going to be captured from the force they were trying hard to elude. The soldiers cuffed all the rebels, put bags over their heads, and transported them to a special prison. These prisons had been emptied when the Exalter offered inmates the great pardon. Now these emptied prisons were slowly filling up and becoming overcrowded again, just like before. The only difference this time is that none of the men and women behind bars ever faced a jury. Young men and women were not spared in this global sweep, as they were in the same facilities as adults. There was no mercy, and if someone thought prison food was bad, at least it was given three times a day. These people ate once a day.

These days were strange for everyone. The word *"survival"* came to mind, as everyone was trying to survive in some shape or form. Derogates who were fortunate enough to find the NOVA center survived in fear of not being discovered. Many of the former Derogates wondered if they had to believe in this Only in order to survive the dark storms of life. Former Knowers had even turned on the Exalter, and now, they were trying to survive on the opposite side of the corrupted laws. And then, many people all over the world just didn't care; they took the incision in order to get what they needed economically.

They thought, What could be so harmful about a little incision, compared to a beheading? The animals in the wilderness were surviving by attacking men and women who weren't prepared to fight back. Large packs of wild dogs and coyotes were feared the most because of their overpowering numbers. Only a handful of people didn't have to worry about surviving. These people included the Exalter and the Seer, of course, but also Tyranus, Granite, and Jupiter. The Exalter made sure his more important Circle soldiers and their families were lavishly attended to, but with such shortages, he had to be careful about making empty promises. A large delivery of supplies was distributed thanks to the fully stocked warehouses Cedro left behind. The Exalter consumed the inventory, as expected. The rainfall was helping to bring a greenish color back to the earth, but growing and harvesting time was at its end. The rain had not hit the right window of opportunity.

The day was clear and crisp, with barely any wind, and the temperature was just right. Tyranus was taking advantage of the weather outside and practicing his limitations (if you could call having super strength any type of limit). He was also practicing aiming his weapons with the custom-made arsenal made especially for him. Granite likewise was outside, only he was enjoying a swim in the pool at his residence, which looked more like the size of a hotel pool to accommodate this beast of a man. Lastly, Jupiter was fighting drone soldiers and testing out his holographic equipment that even fooled these metallic soldiers. Jupiter took such great pride in his technology versus his strength. He almost wanted to worshiped his technology. His conquering mind used both strength and wisdom to defeat his foes.

As Tyranus continued his drills, something made him stop. The ground beneath him was moving, and he didn't feel in control any longer. The earth cracked and broke as templates shifted. An earthquake was shaking the foundations and bringing down the buildings. Different parts of the ocean and even rivers were starting to create whirlpools, with water sinking in the deep earth's crust. Tyranus gained his footing and looked up in the sky and saw something strange: A large shadow was starting to cast from an incoming object. It first looked to be a large spaceship, and then as it came down faster, it produced a black billowing trail of smoke. The object was a large asteroid, and it was coming in faster and faster.

Granite stopped swimming in his pool when he heard the loud noise; he thought it was a plane flying low. Jupiter heard nothing as he battled more and more drones and concentrated on the use of his technologically sophisticated weapons. Tyranus' eyes widened as he bent his knees in preparation to get out of this thing's path. It was too late, and the large asteroid planted Tyranus deep into the earth as dust blanketed his surroundings. Granite only had time to see the blocking out of the sun as his pool emitted a giant wave around the impact and then drained into the hole, where Granite's dead body lay underneath the asteroid. Lastly, Jupiter didn't hear anything. His sensors picked up the object, and he initiated all his weapons on his armor to be active, but his weapons were not enough to break up this rocket-propelled piece of matter. Jupiter was also impaled into the ground just like the others; they all died instantly.

There was no need to even hold funeral services. These super soldiers were buried in the earth already, with large gravestones marking their final resting place.

Many people had seen these giant asteroids coming into the earth's atmosphere and looked for shelter when none was to be found. How does someone find shelter when even the shelter is shaking, with the ground below it unstable? Those three amazingly distinct asteroids had met their marks, unless it was some type of coincidence. Did the Exalter kill them or what?

Immediately afterward, more meteoroids entered the atmosphere and mixed in with asteroids and meteors, as the earth was showered with falling debris. If people thought the drought was a killer, this was a catastrophe. The dead were not countable, and the injured numbered even more. Many communication systems had also broken down. Some operations were still functional, but the Knowers watched as their guardians powered down. If these metal bodyguards weren't around to protect them, who would? Who could stop the giant dust clouds in the atmosphere and the change in temperature was also very noticeable to all.

All day long, people had been looking to find shelter, as the whole earth seemed to be under attack. Suddenly, they all looked up as smoke and dust was clearing in the air, just like when a fish tank settles after being stirred. Things were clear now, and the sun had gone away, but it was only midday. Where was it? Had an asteroid taken the entire sun out? Was that even possible? The moon showed up and reflected a blood-red color to it. If the sun were gone, then where was the moon getting its light? What was this all about? Things were getting too hard to understand. What in the world was going on besides death, fear, and confusion?

People who were able to came out of hiding. Some cries from those stuck in crumbled buildings were heard, while many were trapped and not heard at all. The layers of rubble insulated the sound so that no one could hear the desperate voices gasping for air. Those who did come out did the same thing: They all looked up to see if it was over. After a false sense of safety, something else appeared in the sky. It was turning out to feel like a Monday when you're late for work and the kids won't cooperate and the car won't start. Everything was going far more than wrong. For those who weren't still in their basements, a second wave of problems was forming in the sky. The earth was being peppered by fireballs from the sky. You might have guessed that the fire wouldn't spread since that great rainfall. However, there were plenty of dried-up sticks, grass, and foliage from the drought. Out of control, fires began to spread as people panicked and tried to put them out. Knowers were yelling at their guardian robots to help them, but the guardians were all powered down. They were of no use now. Instead, the guardians were just large hunks of metal only good for scrap.

A freightliner on the west Pacific Ocean was the only ship in sight. The *Mammoth II* had sustained dents but no holes, believe it or not. The firestorm had taken a toll but not enough to make the call to abandon ship. The ship's captain went out on deck, covered in ash smoke around his face and beard. He looked around at the boat and then checked the scenery with his binoculars. A shadow fell upon the boat, and the captain looked up slowly. An object that was too overwhelming to classify was heading straight toward them. The giant piece of matter hit the sea with an astonishing impact, causing an enormous tidal wave. The *Mammoth II* had been a juggernaut in the ocean until this impact flipped the freightliner belly-up. The crew and the captain had no chance. The force and impact were not humanely possible to survive. Great numbers of other ships were destroyed in the entire world, with no one able to rescue the few survivors. It would be more than likely that the sharks would make their own rescue attempts.

At first, all that was known was that an object had landed in the Pacific. Water taken from that ocean was purified for use from that point on, but those who drank it grew very sick for weeks. Who would have thought this alien object had spread some alien contagion that resembled such a bitter taste? People think that everything should be solved at another man's hands. In this type of economy, who had the money to fix an ocean-wide problem? Who was going to dive and find this alien object? More than likely, nothing was going to be done. Not with everything else that was going on. The average citizen didn't know the large alien rock had been the reason for people dying. But the focus point of blame had changed. It used to be the Derogates. Now it was the Exalter and whatever or whoever the real god was. People cursed god in pure hatred and fear in their suffering whether they believed in a god at all or not.

The next days were strange. The entire world had suffered something much worse than a hurricane, tsunami, or tornado. They were attacked from space, and as everyone struggled to clean up, collect the dead, and find the almost-dead, other mysteries unfolded. The sun no longer looked round. A third of the star was missing. So was that of the moon. Even the stars at night did not all burn as bright as they usually did. The sun only shone a third of the day, setting before evening. The moon did the same during the evening.

The universe was becoming unglued, and there had been all this talk about peace in the past. It seemed that men's words were not the final authority. It was getting hard for people to talk about everything and even harder to find help. Some people repented on the street, asking for forgiveness. They asked for forgiveness from whatever god was really god. Others simply asked for forgiveness from the Exalter, as if he had been the one who created the global punishment. Other people began making gods out of different material, including outlawed precious metals. Wood statues were formed and people began to worship the idols, hoping for a respite from the catastrophes. Since it happened, most people thought it was what they deserved.

Out of one large hole in the earth, a group of Circle soldiers were encamped at a small base. They looked at one large crater that was smoking. Binoculars showed that the huge crater was literally smoking. Maybe a fallen asteroid or something had been on fire. The commander of the base was given the binoculars, and as he looked on, he noticed something very strange: It looked like a cloud of some type of insect was swarming out of this crater. The outpouring insects looked like the silhouette of a fountain spraying very high and in all directions. The commander was astonished and kept staring. The other soldiers didn't need binoculars to see the spectacular and fearful site. All the men started heading toward the doors of the base to get inside.

The innumerable wings made a terrifying sound, and before the men got to the door, the swarm was upon them. The flying insects stung them with their tails. At first, the soldiers thought the insects were aliens. They resembled locusts, but there was so much more. The heads of the locusts were shiny, like gold on the top. Each insect's face was shaped like a person's face (without the color of flesh). Their hair was long in comparison to their body size. The soldiers swatted at the would-be locusts, which were armored somehow; the men couldn't kill them. Worse the familiar resemblance in such a form was so incredibly scary. They sought refuge in the base to nurse their wounds from all the stinging.

One soldier voiced his opinion: "I mean, are ya kidding me? What kind of sci-fi experiment was that? Those things weren't tryin' to eat us. They were attacking us just to attack us. Where did they come from?"

All those questions, but no one had any immediate answers. A news report that night gave out information for people to be very careful and stay inside until the problem could be addressed. Many of the news channels said the same thing. However, most channels had switched off completely, since the major satellites were destroyed. It would have been a joke to pretend that land lines were still intact.

The reports continued, "There is a new developing story this evening. The rebel population has once again unleashed an attack on all of the Knowers and against the mighty Exalter. The rebels have created a terrible race of genetically modified locust. The chief scientist from the Triune now joins us live."

The scientist said, "These cloned locusts have unusual characteristics, and they have been described as relentless. I examined a sample locust and can tell you they are very hard to kill indeed. These clones have stinging tails like a scorpion. I am working on a repellent, but even if nothing works, there is good news. For some reason, call it juvenile mistakes of inexperienced scientists, I have discovered that these locusts only have a life span of five months. Now I know that sounds awful, but this species is unable to procreate; either way we will destroy them."

People couldn't believe all the bad news. When was it going to stop? None of it made sense, and even worse, people were starting to seek their own ways of secret worship. Vast majorities of people were praying to their statue gods, asking for mercy and for the plague of the locusts to stop. Those bitten by the locusts underwent different scales of suffering. Some experienced sharp burning and tingling at the sting site. Other had numbness, swollen tongues, difficulty breathing, trouble swallowing, and even seizures. None of the stings were fatal, however. They just suffered enough to want death, but they did not get it. That is when a vast majority started to curse the gods or whoever was responsible for this.

$\mathcal{C}$hapter 36

Two guards were standing outside the Triune headquarters, which had not suffered much damage from the rain shower from space. A man in regular gear started walking up to the Circle soldiers. There was nothing out of the ordinary about this man, as they watched him coming from a short distance. This was Talique's chance. This was his perfect timing in the wake of the confused aftermath. Hopefully, Knower devices would be glitching out or something. Talique walked up to the soldiers, and they looked at him and waited for his hand.

One soldier spoke up, saying, "All this craziness going on around here, you had better just get inside."

Talique responded, "The holy Exalter takes and gives, and now we have to keep going on with our work. For me, unfortunately, that means digging through investigations behind a desk and also scanning boring surveillance video."

With that, he stretched out his right hand, and the soldier made a closed-lip smile. *Beep.* The scan went through, and he was on his way.

The second soldier butted in, "Hey, wait a minute. That scan didn't identify."

Talique stopped with his right hand on the door handle to the building. The first soldier spoke out, "Oh, Brother Hawkins, this junk's been acting up since the quakes and comets. Just go on through, man; we know you're good. Besides, we can't always rely on technology. And what, Hawkins, you think this guy killed someone for his chip or something? Yeah, right."

Hawkins said lowly, "I'm just saying ..."

Talique laughed confidently, although he was nervous inside as he stepped through the doorway. Now where was it? He looked around as he walked, trying to look as if he belonged. After minutes that seemed like hours, he found the room. The door was labeled "In the Dark." Talique used his hand again to open the door. The two soldiers hadn't realized that he had used special adhesives and some coloring to smooth that chip against his skin, with the mold covering it. There was no way he was going back to having a chip again. Talique entered the room and went over to the computer. He had learned a lot from Nicolai and from the waterfall base, and his forefathers had kept up with sophisticated technology. Using passwords he viewed from his holographic wrist band, he accessed the Knower mainframe and typed in what he came for.

He typed in as he looked at the screen, spelling it out with his finger taps: D-E R-O-G-A-T-E P-R-I-S-O-N-S. At least, that was what these vacant prisons were now being called, although some inmates were not Derogates. Some prisoners broke the law or simply refused to take the chip; they really didn't believe in anything. You would think they would at least take the chip and lie in order to avoid punishment, but they didn't. The locations popped up all over the screen, and Talique took out his inviso-device. This special device uploaded information without detection. The download started, and Talique started to sweat. He was thinking about all the people he could help if he just knew their location. They needed to be saved from the Exalter, from suffering, and from eternal death. It was all too obvious that things were happening quickly, and there wasn't much time before the other signs were going to take place. He felt the burden of the lives on his mind and in his heart. But there wasn't time to dwell on that he had to focus on getting out of there. The inviso-device was done, and now he had to get out of there, with the mission accomplished.

Talique walked out the doorway and started toward an exit. He couldn't go out the way he came and knew he had to avoid other checkpoints. Knowers had many checkpoints. Talique began to walk to the back of the building, and he even had an eerie feeling while passing by the Exalter's office doors.

In that office, the Exalter himself looked outside his door sensing something down the hall and made a squinting, unpleasant face.

He picked up his telecom and snapped, "I want a full sweep of this place and a lockdown until further notice. Get it done now."

Lights flashed, and a medium tone alarm sounded. Talique opened his lungs for a deep breath and found a great spot for the exit. He pulled out the other gadget he had with him, pointed it toward a large glass window, and pushed the button. A large red circle formed on the glass; it glowed deep red and started eating through the window. This was a laser pulse device used only by special military and not easy to find. However, Talique's secret base had food, and it was amazing what some Circle soldiers were willing to sacrifice in order to have food and water.

Talique went to push through the glass, but it didn't budge. "Oh great," he said out loud as he realized this was no ordinary glass. The windows were imperviable, almost everything-proof. The laser ate only one fourth through this glass, so Talique gave it another go, hoping that the little device had enough juice to get him out of there. A second time, and still nothing, as the glass didn't budge. You would never guess the window was six inches thick when looking straight through it.

Talique gave another go for the third time, as the sound of heavy soldier boots was heard in the distance. The laser sputtered a little bit, and Talique turned it off and blew on it to cool it down. He knew this fourth attempt was all he had. He put the laser up again, hoping that he could align the circle in the exact same place for a last try.

"Please, Only, let this work."

The circular piece shifted but didn't fall out of the window. Talique pushed hard, and the circular piece fell against the outside wall with a hard thud. He jumped through and began a hard run, with the intent of reserving strength if he needed a quicker sprint. He was sure the Knowers wouldn't stop until they got him. And there they were, only thirty yards behind him on his trail.

Talique ran and ran as fast as he could. All the Circle soldiers ran behind him, getting closer and closer. A single soldier had a better idea on the top of the Triune headquarters. He switched his sniper rifle to sonic, zoomed in on Talique, and pulled the trigger with pleasure.

The concentrated sonic blast smacked Talique in the back like a car wreck, as he went to the ground with the wind knocked out of him. He was recovering as the soldiers jogged up to him and secured the perimeter. He was done for. He knew his attempt had been in good standing with the Only, and he could die for his attempt; he accepted that.

The soldier came over to Talique and said, "Kneel, you trash. We have our orders for you, and they will be followed. Now tell me what you were doing in there."

Talique spoke, out of breath, saying, "I serve the Only. I will not answer any of your questions. Go ahead and do what you are going to do."

The soldier clenched his jaw and was disgusted by Talique's comment, as no one ever spoke boldly like that or even mentioned the name of the Only.

"Your days are over, you Derogate scum." The soldier drew his rifle up and began to aim down his sights at Talique's head.

Soldiers around started acting uncomfortable, and the leading soldier noticed as he looked around at his men. All around him, men began stripping off their armor and uniforms while wailing. The soldier just held his gun and looked around in confusion.

"What is wrong with all of you?" After he said that, he began to feel the red sores forming on his own body under all the armor. Then he dropped his gun and went with his left hand to the middle of his back, as he began to wail himself. He tore off his uniform as these ugly red sores were growing on his skin, like seedlings rising up for the sun. All the soldiers were completely distracted with the pain and cried to make it go away.

Talique looked around and realized that he was not in danger anymore. He stood up. The leading soldier tried to stop him, and Talique pushed the man down; the fall must have aggravated the man's sores, because he yelled again, as if the pain had increased. Talique made his way through the thicket, and thanks to his elaborate plan, his men already had his position. All he had to do was get to the nearest road; he would be evacuated back to his sanctuary and out of this misery. Talique knew what the sores were and why they appeared. None of the soldiers knew where it had come from; they tried to ease the pain of the sores, which were extremely sensitive.

Some were yelling, "That Derogate infected us with some airborne disease. I'm gonna kill him. They're all gonna die."

Chapter 37

"So here he comes," Kiyana said in a low voice.

Janae looked out the window and saw a very nicely dressed man walking to the front door. Behind the man, the street looked like it had been through a blender due to the meteor showers. There had been rumors of a new disease that caused horrible sores, but so far, no one in their household had it. The soldiers seemed to be the first ones getting the sores, for some reason. Janae was excited that amid all the strange things that were going on, maybe something normal might happen. The man walked into the house, looked around, and surveyed the new wives he would take on.

He was medium height with an unfitting mustache and a refined walk. He was the snobby type with his nose in the air above that mustache. He was older than Janae expected, maybe in his late thirties. His sideburns were trimmed thin, and a haircut that needed product in it displayed his brown hair. His outfit revealed that he was a tad bit overweight, no doubt from lavished living.

"I am Boenger Meeds, and I will be the new headmaster of this house. The divorce from Nicolai Turner has been finalized. This is my first house as a headmaster. Unlike the traitor who occupied this space, I expect some things around here. I expect that the food and rations we have will be split fairly and that you will cook for me. I expect the devotion of you all, and in turn, you will have my devotion. These times are unclear, and men have made promises that sound good until you see the end results. I am not here to make promises, but I will do the best I can if you all give me your best in return."

Boenger walked over to Kiyana and said, "I expect that you will prepare dinner for me at six o'clock then."

He then walked up to Janae, who felt nervous, even though the other three wives did not (or at least they didn't show it). "I expect that you will meet me in my quarters at nine o'clock this evening. It is time to sanctify this household."

Janae just kept her head up, and Boenger went to take his things into the bedroom. What a twisted little world they all were looking at. This Boenger was trying to make a controlled lifestyle as if nothing was going on outside those walls.

Janae could only think about that evening in her bedroom. She knew that this man had probably body shared with other women and didn't see her as very special. She pumped herself up to ignore all of that and pretend like she was special. After all, didn't Boenger pick her out of four other women?

Yeah, he did, so there was no doubt she already had his favor. Now all she needed to do was please him and make him feel special. Making him feel special would in turn give her the love she had sought for so long. This was her new identity now, after all the mess. Not even over a year ago, she would have been serving Knowers and sleeping in that trash mud hut. Now, she had things, even when the world around her was falling apart. Janae could feel the world falling apart, as if it were all going to come to an end.

She thought, One day, I will wake up, and this will all be over. For now, I am going to live life to the fullest and get all I can get. I'm not going back to that misery of being a Derogate, no matter what.

That night, after dinner, Janae did exactly what she was told and reported to Boenger's quarters. Afterward, he dismissed her back to her own quarters. She had never even had a boyfriend relationship with a man, so this was a big deal for her.

She said softly, "Please, Boenger, may I sleep in the bed here with you? I won't be in the way, and it would make me feel better to be held by the man I am to serve. It would also make you feel better to have someone to hold onto you."

Boenger looked like he was sorting it out as he lay under the sheets, expecting to go to sleep. Janae acted before he could say no. She nestled herself in the bed and put his arm around her. She held his hand, and even this man who seemed like such a brick wall, he himself felt comforted. It was as if Boenger was trying to fight having a close connection, for some reason. Many of the Knowers were that way. A certain desensitizing, where a Knower would stay away from real feelings that made them feel vulnerable or convicted. Why were they all keeping their best part to themselves? Were they afraid of actually loving one person and not the others? Their Wednesday church settings taught only greed and quick pleasures. And no matter what, to serve the Exalter.

Janae wasn't thinking about any of that. All she could do was savor the moment, where she felt she had a purpose. She felt like she was being loved by a real man. She felt like she was special. She was glad to be somewhere that had a fit for her outside of those black suet villages. As she fell asleep, she was happy for the first time in a long time.

Boenger, on the other hand, was thinking about how lame this girl was; the first thought in his mind was how annoying it was to have her in bed with him. He wanted to spread out in that bed and he didn't want to talk. He didn't want to cuddle. He was just like the rest of the Knower headmasters. Most of the thoughts they had start with the letter "I."

Chapter 38

The holy Exalter's voice echoed in the prison's loudspeakers: "You all are going to have your day of judgment. Of that, you can most definitely be sure. I gave you my love, gave you the chance to serve me, and even gave you the chance to come back to me. I would have forgiven you for your sins against me, but you still did not repent. You all are evil and destined for the eternal pit. I will make an example of you all on my designated day. On the anniversary of my seventh year in power here on earth, you will all be executed on the halovision. You will have no more chances to share my kingdom."

Servantés had begun crying through the Exalter's speech. Now he let go of the grasp he had on his prison cell bars and fell to his knees as he continued to weep aloud. Tyrisha and Shay Lynn were in the cell next to Servantés and could easily hear him.

Tyrisha tried to comfort him, saying, "Don't worry, Servantés, this is not the end. Just like I told you all, there is a reason for all this. You will not die and go to the pit. You will be in heaven with the Only, and you will finally know what real peace is."

He kept crying and then said, "You don't understand. It was my fault. We got captured because of me. I had the incision in my hand,

and when the soldiers loaded me into the helicopter, they thanked me for the signal. It was me, all me."

Tyrisha replied kindly, "Servantés, you didn't know that would transmit a signal. Don't blame yourself for one second. You have to understand that everything happens for a reason; even though we think we are in control, the Only leads our path. I know it doesn't make sense now, but it will. The Only will show us. Maybe the Only brought me here to spread his word to people in prison. Maybe this is a test that you need, Servantés, so that you can believe. You haven't taken the incision out yet, and there must be a reason for that. The point is, we have to trust the Only and understand he is in control. If everything was your fault or my fault, it would mean that we were under the delusion that we have control over our lives. We can't blame a mistake we made on ourselves because if we knew we were going to make it, we would have chosen differently. There is a lesson to learn here, so cheer up."

Servantés sat there for a couple minutes in complete silence. Tyrisha walked over and sat on her bunk while Shay Lynn was lying down on the top bunk, just staring at the ceiling. A large weight was off their shoulders, at least. They didn't have to worry about being captured or who was around the corner. They weren't looking around for Circle soldier helicopter scans or vehicle patrols. Even though they were captured, that was the only real fear they had, and that part was over.

"You know they took my boy and wife away from me?" Servantés continued. "Our boy was only twelve months old, and they wanted to give him the incision. I didn't like that idea, and neither did my wife. I said I wasn't going to allow it. We went off into the unknown and were doing just fine, despite all the dangers out there. My father had taught me how to live off the land, just like his ancestors, and I am glad he did."

Servantés was a modern man, and his jaw structure and black hair indicated he may be of Indian ancestry. He looked to be in the prime of his life, despite the recent circumstances. He looked deeply depressed, and his dark features only enhanced his emotions.

"I went out to the woods to get firewood, after leaving them hidden in a small shelter I built. I was only gone forty-five minutes, gathering wood and wishfully scouting for some dinner. When I came back, the shelter was destroyed and boot tracks were all around it. I looked closely to the tracks, and they were the footprints of Circle soldiers. Oh, my beautiful Rosalea, my son Alejandro… Why did I ever leave you both for so long? I can't forgive myself for it, and it's all I think about. Now here I am, locked up in here. How will I ever find them? Will I ever know what happened to them?"

Shay Lynn began crying silently up on the top bunk, listening to Servantés. Tyrisha took it all in and knew even in the most perilous situations, the Only would come through. He promised that he would protect and provide, and she knew for sure it was true.

She said, "That story is not easy to hear, let alone be the one who lived it. But I have no doubt that you need the Only now, more than any other time in your life. I believe that if you ask him into your heart, believing that his son died on the cross, and seek forgiveness for your sins, that all will go well for you and your family. He will give you the gift of his holy spirit, and he will guide you. Let's face it: None of us can do anything about your family. However, relying on the Only, who has made all, will make a difference."

Servantés wasn't sold on this speech entirely, but what did he have to lose? His pride was gone. He had lost his family, and Rosalea had been his everything. He lived for her. He loved for her. With the addition of young Alejandro, the importance just multiplied. He recalled what he would tell her every Monday: "Here is a beautiful flower for a beautiful woman on the start of another beautiful week together." He would say that as he handed her a pink flower. Pink was her favorite color, and Rosalea would chuckle and kiss Servantés as they enjoyed their time together.

"Tyrisha," he finally said, "you have been very kind to me, for someone who just happened to walk into this cave. I will have to talk with your Only later about all you have said. There is no denying that I can do nothing like this. There is also no denying that things here on earth are very wrong; when I listened to you in the cave, so much made sense, and it feels right somehow. Don't worry about me. I have faith to see my boy and Rosalea again, and that is what keeps me going. Thank you for your concern. Now you two just get some rest, and I will do the same."

Tyrisha smiled, turned away from Servantés' cell, and stood up, looking at Shay Lynn.

"So, Tyrisha, what do we do now?" Shay Lynn asked; she believed the experience Tyrisha had told her about, with seeing the angel, so she looked for guidance from her.

"We pray about everything, Shay Lynn. We pray and know we are here for a reason. Besides, just look at all the signs we have seen already. I am not sure how much longer everyone here on earth has."

Shay Lynn always had a good attitude and shot back cheerfully, "Well, sure, I can pray, that's easy. And yeah, it seems like the world is going to end soon. But for now, even this jailbird cot feels good, and a pillow under my head sure beats whatever rocks and brush I could find outside to lay my head on. I need some rest.

Chapter 39

Leviticus and Nicolai were sitting near the entrance, viewing the new people coming in. They were discussing the same old stuff about the world falling apart and what that meant. Then Nicolai spotted a very disturbing scene. Could it be her? It wasn't. Oh yes, it was.

What was Xyla doing at the gate? Nicolai said, "I don't want you to panic, but that is Xyla over there, going through the scanners."

Leviticus stood up quickly; he couldn't believe it. "What? The same Xyla who locked up my mother? She deserves to die for what she did."

Nicolai grabbed Leviticus by the shoulder and sat him back down gently. "No, no, we need to approach this very delicately."

They walked up to the commander in charge of the entrance and told him about their concerns. Nicolai informed the guard that this woman was a Knower, and an evil one, at that. He told the commander how she had imprisoned Leviticus's mother in her basement and that she could not be trusted.

After a moment, Xyla noticed both of them, and her eyes grew wide as she attempted to remain composed. She was very nervous about this indeed; she didn't know who Nicolai was talking with. There was no doubt that he was working on destroying her first impression.

"You horrible person," Leviticus said. "How could you do it? This woman took my mother from me. She took away my father's wife, just because of jealousy. She is evil and can't be trusted. She needs to die for what she has done. Don't let her go outside those walls. She is a spy; lock her up."

Nicolai stared at Xyla's face as he watched the scene unfold; instead of anger, he only felt sympathy for Leviticus.

The commander told both of the men to calm down and said that an investigation would be conducted.

Amongst the confusion, Xyla said, "He is right. I did take his mother away from him and his father. I was selfish, jealous, and envious. I also used to be the wife of a self-absorbed man. He and his other wives were killed by the Knowers. I knew he was involved in illegal smuggling, but I didn't want to lose all that I had. I narrowly escaped and joined up with others who I was told could get me here. Look at my hand. I don't have the incision inside anymore. I don't have to depend on the government to take care of me. This awful thing has opened my eyes and brought me to myself, where I can see who I was becoming. I am very sorry for all the pain I caused you, sir. Please forgive me, and I will someday hopefully forgive myself. It doesn't matter what we were outside these walls. We all are here now, and I need a new start. Isn't that why we all are here? For a new start, for hope, and for the truth?"

Xyla had done very well at listening to those trusted few who would lead new people into the waterfall sanctuary. She listened to them as they spoke about the Only and his commandments and what there is to receive. She was playing a great role and had only this minor mission to complete before she could have her future secured.

Leviticus repeated, with anger in his tear-filled eyes, "Don't trust her."

Chapter 40

Talique had been back for days. Just as Nicolai went in the elevator downward, so did Xyla. Xyla heard a man talking in the distance.

"From what I got, this location is close. It will be very simple to use double pulse rounds to break through the walls. Then, we can make the multiple extractions and get out of there before we find ourselves with any dangerous tails on us."

The door opened, and Talique waved his hand to make the screen disappear. Xyla only caught a glimpse of what looked like some type of structure from an aerial view. She had told her story, and it was too easy. When someone is full of compassion and wants others to switch to the right path, it can be dangerous. The accepting ones are sometimes blinded by their eagerness. And in turn, the unwanting ones are all too eager to be accepted, so they can get on with their deceitful plans. Xyla was released and put in general population, although she was being monitored very closely.

A week went by, and Nicolai and Leviticus had nothing to do with Xyla. They stayed away from her, and she didn't mind one bit. She was too busy trying to convince the instructors that she was going to go out the doors and bring people back. She was learning the holy book of the Only and even could cite some easy verses. After only a week, she was ready to get outside of these wretched walls full of these happy-go-lucky, brainwashed morons. All these people knew about was serving each other, forgiving each other, and giving thanks.

Yuck, she was done with all of this. She was an expert liar. She lied about lying and used lies to get what she wanted. She had done so well that after only a week, those in authority allowed her to go outside with a small group to look for stragglers who needed shelter. One day, Nicolai and Leviticus were looking on as Xyla's group was ready to take off.

Nicolai said, "It is good that she is leaving. Maybe she won't come back."

Leviticus replied, "Yeah, but that's what I'm afraid of. Say she doesn't come back, but instead, a whole Circle soldier army does, with the intent of killing us all and destroying this place. Then what? Certain people deserve forgiveness. But you forgive them and then get them out of your life because they won't change. She is that type. I want to be as far away from her as I can."

That night outside the walls of the city, Xyla decided it was time to make her move. She held her stomach and began making sounds of pain. She then began to walk into the woods.

A guard said loudly, "Xyla, where are you going?"

She replied, "Something is very wrong with my stomach. This is really embarrassing for me. I have the worst stomach cramps. It must be the switch over to freeze-dried food. Ohhhh, I can't hold it. I gotta go. I'll be back."

The soldier felt grossly uncomfortable and raised his voice a little bit as she walked away, stammering, "I'll wait for you right here."

Xyla didn't waste any time. That trip to the Exalter's dentist had not been for just a cleaning. He had given her a fake tooth. She reached in her mouth and took off the lead-lined hollow crown on her tooth. Inside was a small device with a tiny switch. She used a small nail file to flip the switch on. The holographic display came up to alert the Exalter that she was leaving the rebel site. She looked at the holographic display and saw she had six miles to travel. About three and a half hours later, she reached her mark. A small vehicle sat in the woods, right where she had left it.

She tried to start the vehicle but the ignition did not work. Was this the act of the Only? Was it a disturbance from the meteor showers? Why now? Why this time? With no other type of device or communications from the vehicle, she was in trouble. She pushed the ignition button time and time again, with no luck; she was getting angrier by each attempt.

What in the world was that sound? Xyla heard a dog barking and some strange pitter-patter noise. She got into the vehicle and locked the door. As the dawn grew brighter, she became quite nervous in the car; after a few minutes, she heard a loud whimper. She looked around but saw nothing. She turned on her little guidance beacon that was in her hand and tried to shine it outside the car but still could see nothing. She looked around again, and this time, a quick motion scared her deeply.

A large dark dog had barked and placed his front paws on the window of the vehicle. The dog's overgrown nails tapped hard on the glass. More dogs surrounded the vehicle and started jumping on it, trying to get at Xyla. She was scared but knew that the wild dogs couldn't break into the car. There was another loud roar, and the dogs scattered away. From the front windshield, Xyla could see a very big, dark animal trotting slowly toward her; it was a bear!

The bear approached the car, stood on his back legs, and let out a large roar. The bright moonlight gave Xyla a hope if she had to escape on foot. At least she would be able to see where she was going. The bear sniffed around the vehicle and must have decided the windshield looked easy. He put his weight on the windshield, grunting and jumping on the car with all his weight. The glass buckled but did not break; Xyla was completely shaken and trembling with fear.

Like a balloon popping, the little windshield finally cracked open, and the bear began to reach in. As soon as it broke, Xyla instinctively opened the door and began to run. As she sprinted away, the bear looked back and took off after her. Her escape succeeded, but then one of the dogs jumped on her back, knocking her to the ground. The dog sank his teeth into Xyla's back, and she managed to shake him off as she shrieked in pain. The pack circled in closer to Xyla, who looked from side to side at the last images she was most likely to see on earth; she started crying hysterically and saying, "No, go away. This can't be happening. Please, someone help!"

Another roar rang out as the bear reappeared; both the dogs and Xyla looked up to see the massive bear on the ridge. He began to run down the hill, stirring up dust in his wake, and the dogs once again scattered in fear. Xyla was badly injured and could only watch and listen as the bear approached her, growling. She was more than petrified, and then she was no more, after the bear followed his natural instincts and went for her throat to drain her life force.

It was a bitter ending for Xyla. She had thought herself a dominant predator amongst those weaker men in her games. She never factored she would be outplayed.

Chapter 41

Dr. Gerzak was looking at the screen and finally gave the couple the answer they were waiting for. The doctor was balding with silver hair and wore his readers to look through the couple's paperwork. He had green eyes that he always made sure were looking into the eyes of his patients giving them the full attention instead of the regular in and out treatment. He didn't have to wear one of those white lab coats, uniforms but he must have liked to. He even wore nice shoes. It must have made him feel normal like before. There all three of them stared at the screen in the women's center. This women's center was the same secret city affiliated with the NOVA establishment in that waterfall cave.

"Congratulations," he announced, "you are going to have a little baby girl."

Pascual, the husband, smiled and said, "Oh, Gems, can you believe it? This is so great!"

Pascual smiled with and looked intent at Gems with his dark blue eyes. He lowered his head to Gems and his hair moved a little bit down his head and somewhat in his eyes. He looked like a country music star, all right. Pascual was so happy despite the terror outside those walls. The woman that he loved was pregnant with his child. This was amazing, and his pregnant wife looked even more beautiful with her baby bump.

Gems grinned also, staring right back with her hazel eyes returning the connection. But then her smile faded as she turned to the doctor. She had been so concerned about the development of her baby, despite the great care she got since arriving at the center. This was her first pregnancy, and she felt clueless. She seemed unsure of herself and raised her eyebrows in concern.

She asked, "Doctor, do you think we are stupid for trying to have a baby? I mean, look around at all of this horrible mess. What could we do? No one has access to spawn blockers, so here we are. But this little one didn't have a choice, and I fear she won't make it."

The doctor turned the monitor back on and moved the scanner over the partially developed baby. For a moment, he watched the screen along with Gems and Pascual.

Dr. Gerzak said, "This baby didn't ask to be made, that's true; she just knows that she simply is. The love you both have for each other has created this youngster. The Only has favored you both with a hope of fresh air in these times of judgment. This little one certainly has more than a chance; don't ever doubt that."

The couple seemed pleased with the answer, and after setting up their next appointment, Gems and Pascual exited.

Dr. Gerzak's nurse, who had overheard the conversation, asked him, "Do you really believe there is such hope for humanity, even now?"

Dr. Gerzak replied, "Mankind is evil at heart and always will be, until the very end of the new beginning. We start out so innocent, until we learn so much, and then we learn what we don't have and what we think we want. The knowledge of evil gives us the capacity to be evil. Everyone starts with a cognitive understanding of right and wrong."

The nurse listened with surprise. The doctor usually gave short answers, keeping his talk to the minimal. However, she could tell there was more winding up there in his head than he let on.

"People keep control of emotions and greed until things become desperate," he continued. "In desperate times, they would kill you to make their hunger pangs go away, and we've seen that. The lost are all absolutely greedy at heart and want control, power, and some form of happiness. But we all have that capability. As the generations have kept coming, it seems there are fewer people with interpersonal skills. They are desensitized and feel no remorse for their behavior, no matter how abnormal, if such a thing exists anymore."

Dr. Gerzak let out a big breath, like he was releasing all his stress. He then stood up and concluded, "The evolution compliments basic sociopathic feelings, allowing no empathy to penetrate. You ask if there is hope for humanity, even now. The answer is, there is absolutely no hope for us, by ourselves. That is, unless we have the Only in our life. Without Him, everything is a waste of time. Their good works will not matter when weighed against their bad at the judgment chair. The only hope we have is for him to make all wrongs right and for those who are blind to someday see."

Chapter 42

Servantés slept peacefully on his thin, foul-smelling mattress. While he was sleeping, a series of painful red blisters appeared on his skin. He woke up in complete agony and began scratching the bumps. He jumped out of his cot and turned on the dim light. Opening up his shirt revealed that these sores were everywhere, and there seemed to be no escaping the pain.

"Ugh, I am so tired of this," he said. "I am tired of all the awful things that have happened to me since I had this incision put in. I don't deserve this. What have I done? I didn't do anything."

Servantés felt around under the bottom cot and located the rusted-out bolt and nut he had found earlier; they were loose enough to be unscrewed by hand. He wasted no time and began rubbing the end of the bolt forcefully on the floor in a back and forth motion. Every so often, he would turn the bolt and continue filing, as he perspired from the painful sores and the manual mission he was on.

Finally, he had honed that bolt into a thin, sharp tool. Servantés used it to pierce the skin of his right hand; he had lived with that chip for long enough. People had gone to prison because of him and that chip. His wife, Rosalea, had been taken away because of that chip. He kept working at the cut until he was able to pull the chip out, along with the surgical wire attached to it. He took that bloody chip out and then rinsed it off to look at it. He stared at it and then used his weight to break the chip in two. He sat down and began to cry. He looked like a broken man you would see on a corner, begging for money, like back in the old days.

He cleared this throat and said, "Listen, I am not a man who ever thought I needed help. But I am coming to you now and asking for your help. I am asking you to forgive me of my sins, and you know I believe in you now. I have to believe there is more than me. I have to believe that my Rosalea and my son will come back to me. I choose to believe that your son died on the cross and was raised back to life with your power. I accept the gift of the helping spirit. Thank you for forgiving me, and please show me what hope is again."

Servantés took a deep breath, and as he did so, he felt funny. He looked down at his legs, and the sores were literally disappearing right in front of his eyes. He felt his skin, in some small measure of disbelief. He knew right there and then that the Only was real. He knew he had a special purpose, although he didn't know what it was at all.

Servantés walked slowly over to the sink. He took the sliver of soap and began to clean off the blood that had dried on his skin. As he cleaned the wound, he felt cleaner in a spiritual sense. He felt better than ever as he looked at this new man in the mirror.

Chapter 43

The small squad of Circle soldiers had worked their way through several convoys and now faced the beautiful Arabian Sea. Morgan, Smith, Porter, Rodriguez, and Fields had been together for over three and a half years now and really knew each other. They all had their unique ways that made a good balance for the team. It sure is something how long it takes people to get used to each other and let themselves be known to others. The small unit had some downtime, and they were going fishing, as their food supply was getting depleted.

Smith took advantage of the silence to get in a comment: "Why don't you bunch of Momma-pleasers go out there and find us some dinner? Maybe do like the locals and just throw some dynamite out there and see what floats up. Better yet, we can tie up Porter and drag him behind a rowboat as bait. He's small enough. That'll work."

Porter rebutted, "Go duct tape your mouth Smith and jump off the pier with a bowling ball strapped to your ankles, Smith."

Morgan interjected, "Calm down, Sallies, this here fishing pole is gonna scoop us up some grub."

Morgan cast his line, and they chatted for a while until the fishing pole began to tug. Morgan motioned for Fields to take the pole and reel in the catch.

Rodriguez teased Fields, "We gonna be here all night with this gringo trying to reel in anything bigger than a minnow. Just wind it clockwise. You know clock wise mane. You should know this. Your people use clocks to tell them when its time to stuff their face with some double cheeseburgers. Aye, this strange temperature drop that happens around here is bugging me. At least it makes the sores hurt less, being cold. Ugh, frío."

Morgan said, "We already talked about this. Just scratch 'em until they bleed out and scab over. Or if you are a real man who doesn't care about his appearance, just cauterize the sores. I used my cig to burn one sore that was getting the best of me. I feel like I am starting to learn to live with it, if that's possible."

Fields spent a good half-hour reeling fighting with that line, and then they saw something splash to the surface.

Fields looked out and asked, "What is that, a dolphin?"

Morgan studied, "Close: It's a finless porpoise, pretty boy, and dinner is dinner, even if it looks like it should be in a zoo."

Smith had scouted around and found a good place further inland to start a fire. He went back to the shore and told the men he had a fire started so they all could warm up. Fields put the pole in the sand, and they reinforced the pole so that it was secure; they had decided to let the porpoise wear itself out, fighting the line. After warming up at the fire, the men went back to the beach, looking forward to a hot, protein-packed dinner. They were tired of the food supplies they had on them, like regeneration drinks and nasty calorie gel packs. Fields took the rod and felt like he had to finish it. The marker on the fishing line revealed that there was less than thirty five feet left of line out there, and they could hear the splashing of the porpoise.

Smith snapped, "C'mon, Fields, what did you do, diarrhea your pants? Smells disgusting out here."

All the men noticed the foul smell in the air and decided to turn on their flashlights, which was something, because they wouldn't light a match unless it was absolutely needed. If they could build a fire from dried materials and not use matches, they would. They were trained minimalists.

The men were amazed at what they were looking at.

Rodriguez spoke up, saying, "Huh, what is that?"

Morgan walked down to the edge of the water and studied the strange scene. He bent down on his knees and put his hand into the water. He dipped his finger in the red liquid, which should have been salty sea water, and said, "This here appears to be blood, boys."

They all were in disbelief.

"Man, how do you know?" Porter asked.

"I know what blood is, just like the rest of you. Besides, the ocean doesn't dry up on the beach and turn red. Look at this."

Morgan pointed to where the tide had dried out, and there was a dark line of dried blood. He shined his flashlight further out to look at the porpoise. It was obviously struggling to survive in this completely changed ecosystem. Morgan took the fishing rod from Fields and reeled in the dying porpoise. When the porpoise was close enough, it was obvious from the sounds that it couldn't breathe correctly. Morgan drew his sidearm and fired one time, and that was all it took. He took out his survival blade and cut the fishing line.

"Not sure I'd eat this," he said flat, "and he didn't need to suffer like that."

Smith couldn't believe how calm and collected this guy was. "I mean, are you kidding me? Am I missing the movie cameras or something? You act like this is no big deal. This is not normal, man. Do you realize the size of this sea? What is going on here, man? Is this some type of chemical warfare joke gone sour? What's next, lava tsunamis? Dude, I've had it."

The others looked to Morgan for leadership; they were wondering the same thing.

Morgan only said, "I told you all that I studied the forbidden books. I'm not surprised by this. Take it the way you want to. I think it is time for us to find some grub or resort to personal supplies."

He went for his signature move, which was lighting a cigarette after a thought-provoking sentence. He walked away into the darkness; the rest of the men just stared at the ocean in front of them, which had turned to blood. This was impossible. But for a third of the earth, it was very real. A third of the ocean and rivers had turned blood-red, and a third of the sea life had died in the process.

Chapter 44

It was a Wednesday, and the Exalter made his regular appearance in the form of a holographic image on the center stage at the altar. When he appeared, everyone bowed their head in reverence to their god. The hologram was so convincing that it looked like the Exalter himself was at the altar. He began his speech, and this time, everyone knew it was serious. Most telecasts were presented through the halovision, not the holographer. This message was meant to be much more personal. Never before had a preacher's church encompassed the whole world. Small time preachers would have envied this new definition of a mega church. The Exalter's hologram stared at the people, as if he could actually see each temple that was online.

"There are so many lost ones out there," he began. "But how else can you expect them to act without me? They have clung to their nature of disobedient sin, becoming completely corrupt. Just look at what they have conjured up now. I do not gain pleasure in killing a man for his sins. No, I am forgiving, am I not? Haven't I given you all a better life from the many years ago, before I created the Aeon monetary system? Weren't you all killing each other in arguments over who's religion was right or wrong? Terror attacks, violence, greed, and hard work for slavery is what you had. I even went as far to rid the earth of the mentally unstable and place them in special places of solitude to protect you from the impaired. Did I not have every human evaluated through science to determine the withdrawal of normal society? I saved you from the violence."

Every head seemed to nod up and down in agreement to his comments.

"Now, we have a new issue to discuss. The Derogate rebellion has conjured up a chemical weapon against us all. What first seemed to be a very large-scale attack on my world's oceans has now spread into the earth's springs and rivers. Don't they know I can see all? Do they think they are surprising me? No, my children, they do not frustrate me. I have already made preparations. I have many warehouses stocked with healthy, uncontaminated water. Endless pallets of bottled water are waiting to be distributed. And what happens when we consume all of those, you might ask? The answer is coming. My scientists are working to change the contaminated water back to its original form. The Derogate rebels think they can ransom our water for things they want. They hate our freedom, and they want our food, drinks, drugs, and luxury. But they will not have it until they repent for their sins and ask for forgiveness. I tell you the truth, if one of your sons strays from the righteous path and many years go by, do you not rejoice when he comes home to repent? Just the same, I will be glad to get back one lost sheep from my flock."

The background screens came on in each worship temple, showing images of warehouses filled with pallets of water, food, medical supplies, and alcohol.

"Medicine is being distributed to comfort those of you who have been infected by the Derogate rebellion," he continued. "They think that these attacks will bring us down. My people, I do not ask that you serve me for nothing. Without sacrifice, you cannot understand what it is to be thankful. Without trials, tests, and scarce times, how can you ever know what it is to be blessed? Be sure that I will reach for you when you think you are falling down to your grave. I will reach out my replenishing hand and grasp your weak arm as you give up and almost fall down. I will raise you from your former shame and bring you to the peak of your humanity here on earth. When the time comes for my judgment, after you have passed on from this life, I will reward you in heaven for all of your works, be sure of that. The lawbreakers out there thought they had a plan, but I know the path that every man takes. What they have used for evil, I will make for your good.

"I will bring my children together by providing clean water; everyone will work hand in hand to make sure their brothers and sisters are nourished. The sinners thought they would destroy our seas, but my dedicated workers will work to clean and restore that water as well as repopulate the ocean through genetic cloning. These deadly airborne plagues will bring us together in sharing our burdens with each other. Their purpose was to make you weak. But they have made you stronger by bonding in affliction. It is my honor to provide for you when your enemies work to destroy you. No weapon forged in the darkest cave will ever harm a hair on your head.

"Many of you have drifted in your faith in regards to me," he added. "It is perfectly acceptable to be honest with your god and admit your disbelief. I have prepared a special service today. You will find fresh, uncontaminated water in your temples. I want you who doubted me to come forward and rededicate your pledge to me. Don't be afraid to humble yourself and tell me you love me. Your worship leaders take it from here. I am always with you and will never leave you. They will let you down. But I never will. I am eternal and I do not grow hungry, weak, or changed."

The hologram disappeared, and all across the world, the water basins came out with fresh water, as the Knowers came down the aisles, ready for their water baptism to rededicate themselves to their reassuring god.

Chapter 45

Janae stood there in her own temple and was really starting to catch on to all this. She wondered why, when she was with Tyrisha, everything she said seemed to make sense. That was only because no one was there to give the other side of the story. Janae realized that you could be easily swayed by the same suggestions, repeated over and over. This was why all those stupid Derogate children believed what their parents told them. They took the pill just like lab rats, without any question.

Janae switched her thoughts to this new other side. If the Exalter wasn't god, then how could he have known to fill all those warehouses with uncontaminated water? These bad things happening in the world and the itchy bumps on her skin were all part of a spiritual war. Janae was ready to pick up her spiritual sword and fight.

She took Boenger's hand and walked down the aisle of the temple. Out of all the wives she was the only one that seemed so attached to Boenger in such a way. She was ready to get her baptism and to receive forgiveness for her sins. She believed she was making the right choice. All over the world, others followed in Janae's footsteps. They had also doubted the Exalter's authenticity during such times of complete distress. Sure, the Exalter made a great speech that no skeptic reporter could put holes into, but he never talked about the meteor showers or the calamities that followed. How about those terrifying locusts? Perhaps it was just convenient.

Chapter 46

A very light-skinned young soldier stood in his fatigues. He was clean shaven, with a very short military haircut. It was obvious he was no stranger to weight lifting. It was also obvious that he was in some type of trouble and ready to be reprimanded.

"Silas, what happened to that woman Xyla who was lost on the trip?"

The general was not looking so convinced no matter what the corporal was going to spit out. Silas poorly defended himself for the situation. Silas began his reply in English with his French accent incredibly detectable. "Sir, she complained of stomach pains and said she was going to have issues going to the bathroom and needed some privacy. After ten minutes, I checked on her, and she was gone. Our resources weren't large enough to expand a search for her as nightfall was upon us."

The general adjusted his jaw and his top lip edged out. "We can only assume the worst given the report that she could have been a possible traitor. However, I sincerely doubt she will find her way back here considering she had no type of technology on her, and she is frankly a civilian woman alone. I will inform the others. And by the way, this should be your hind end in a blender. You should have had eyes on her.

I don't care if she was having violent diarrhea with loud grunting. This is the security and lives of people living here. We aren't fortunate enough to have a large pool of defenses here so you will remain as you were."

The general was getting a transmission through his ear piece. He listened for a few seconds and said, "Yes, go ahead, I read you."

The woman's voice spoke out, "General, there is a malfunctioning alarm on pump four. A manual check is needed to determine the issue."

The general looked at Silas and spoke, "Roger that. Corporal, get outside with another man and figure out what the issue is on pump four."

The soldier felt just plain stupid, but at least, he had a new task he could accomplish. "Yes, sir, right away." Silas grabbed another guard who was extra at the gate. They exited through the trail behind the waterfall. A small walk downstream was where the pumps were and also they were heavily camouflaged. The soldiers had even seen red blood filled water in other spots, but it wasn't there. Maybe whoever poisoned the water didn't get the supply that fed upstream. At least, that is what all the NOVA members thought.

Silas and another soldier, Wade, headed down the stream. There was pump four and at least it was late enough in the afternoon that the sunlight was shining through the clear sky with still no clouds in sight. Silas looked up and was looking for some mental relaxation.

"Hey, you see the sun, Wade," Silas said.

Wade wasn't even thinking about that. Wade was more of a simple man who had a heart for action. He still had his southern accent to him. He loved to call himself a hillbilly and joked about his long family line of mullets and NASCAR fans.

"It looks so funny with a chunk of it completely gone. Hah, you know what? It looks like that old arcade game, Pacman. You know the little yellow open-faced guy. Oh well, anyway, let's see what we got here."

Wade began his quick spoken language that made your ear listen for interpretation. "Yeah, man, wut you say let's go awn and git outta here den."

The two started taking down the camo-panels. These panels surrounded the piping that went directly into the stream. The panels were thin and literally camouflaged the surrounding, so no one could tell visually that a large pipe was being hidden. These pumps were used for all sorts of the colony's needs. Water would be purified and other water was used for regular needs such as faucets, toilets, and showers. The two looked at the pipe, and their handheld unit that would tell them where the issue was. The instrument beeped, and Silas could tell what the problem was.

Just some type of leak had started. Maybe it was from a temperature change that caused expansion. It didn't matter it just needed fixed.

"Wade, hook me up with a torch and some steel dry powder."

Wade shot back fast, "Check." Wade took off his pack and got the two objects that Silas had asked for. Silas worked and first dried the area and then used the steel dry powder to coat the hole and then used some water and fire to melt a nice sealant any modern plumber would have been proud of. The pair made some other adjustments while they were there and then put the camo-panels back on. Then they started the trip back to the waterfall entrance.

About forty feet from the entrance, Silas looked up again. "Hey, Wade, the sun looks weird today."

Wade replied, "Yeh, summon ain't right bout dat."

Silas went on, "Just look at it. The color is so different than any day I have ever seen. Plus, I can hardly stand to look in that direction even with these shades. It looks intensified or something. I sure hope it doesn't blow up or something nuts. Then we will all have a new very large problem."

Chapter 47

A Knower scientist was working in an underground facility somewhere in United States. Above the facility were complex gadgets and telescopes monitoring the universe. It was even more amazing that the complex instruments had not been destroyed during all the catastrophes. The scientist stared at some screens, double-checking his observations. The thermometers were telling him exactly what the other readings were saying.

He picked up his com and said, "Yes, we have a problem here. There are massive solar flares erupting on the surface of the sun. This is going to cause unpredictable temperatures in scattered locations. It is even possible that gaps through the ozone layer could exist, creating even more danger."

The voice of the Seer answered back calmly, "Thank you, I understand."

The scientist was still listening as he heard the com click off. How could such catastrophic news be answered so calmly like that? This could be the end of the world, and the guy acted like a fuse had blown and just needed to be switched back on.

The scientist was already perspiring from the stress of where his mind wandered from thinking out the scenarios and aftermath of the situation.

Elsewhere in the States, a Knower wingman was talking to his driver Tran; he said, "Wow, it is seriously getting hot. Stop the leviathan so we can get out and strip off this body armor."

Tran replied, "Yeah, we need to get that done quick. This blasted heat killed the air-conditioning."

The men stopped on the side of the road and got out of their vehicle. These leviathans were used to patrol for Derogates and other rebels. The vehicles were equipped with heavy scanning equipment and could even detect small traces of carbon dioxide. Such technology had been used to find those equipped with camo-panels or infrared-deterrent clothing. If you were out there, they would see you, somehow. No rebel weapons could take out the leviathan. You would need a battleship to break through that heavy armor.

The two men stepped out into the road, where they felt the full brunt of the sun's intense heat.

They were outside in the open but felt like they were in a sauna. They began peeling off the armor, sweating heavily. The sun shone down on them without pause, and they sought to escape back into the leviathan for protection, but it was too late, as the metal handles were searing hot, like a sizzling frying pan.

The first soldier cried, "Ouch! The door is scorching hot."

They both looked around, and their survival training kicked in.

Thinking fast, the Tran said, "Listen, we gotta get out of this sun. We need to make a shelter; c'mon."

The other soldier Daygof followed, cursing the sun, along with other curses. Tran walked over to the large slope of the hill off of the road. He used an armor plate from his own body armor to begin digging into the sloped ground.

He hollered over, "C'mon, help me out here, but go slowly. Under this thick dirt, we will find shelter against the cool ground. When nightfall hits, we can get back in the leviathan and get outta here."

The two dug at a steady pace, working together for the same goal of staying alive. The shelter was built, and even though the pair were dehydrated, at least they were out of harm's way, for now.

The intense, scorching heat was felt all over the world. Some people experienced more of it than others. People were being burned by just walking out their door, if they were brave enough. Others were stranded in their vehicles needing to find shelter and instead found a grueling passing from this earth to another. The idea of swimming was finished, as the water was too hot to offer any relief. Roads still intact from all the space showers buckled and cracked, looking like earthquakes had gone through. The few remaining houses in targeted areas warped and collapsed.

There were reports of major bridges buckling and collapsing. This entire event was bearable only for those who had a place to escape. The majority of those in cities sought barely tolerable refuge in their basements. The boredom and trapped feelings were almost as unbearable as the heat. People who were stranded in unsafe places were not as fortunate, succumbing to heat exhaustion and dehydration. It was awful to see people suffering from all the exposure, emotional losses from past devastations, and then watch them vomit from heat exhaustion. It was complete suffering. There was no other word for it.

A majority of people just started cursing the Exalter. Other people cursed whatever god they served. It seemed the same reactions from every disaster were the same from the people on the earth. What about this Exalter, anyway? He was god, right? Maybe they had things in their life before all the horror that they put first. Most of the people put themselves first. They didn't care about anybody else. They didn't even care about the Exalter. They just wanted to do what felt good. They did whatever they had to in order to get by and keep their idols. They didn't bow down on their knees, so to speak; they just wanted to keep their own ideas of sexual satisfaction, lust, greed, jealousy, and addictions. They did whatever they liked in their own lifestyle. They put those things before anyone and anything. Those things were put before the worship of any creator of any type. They were more interested in self-worship. What importance were any of those things when it meant facing the consequences? There was no one to pay to make it go away. No prayer seemed to be working. No cursing seemed to make any difference. Even if you had Aeons you hadn't used to barter for food or whatever, who would take them? Many started asking questions that hadn't ever been raised before. The biggest question was, why?

Chapter 48

"Listen," Talique said, "now is the time."

Others were in slight disagreement because of the unknown.

Talique was working with these officers to convince them it was the time to break the prisoners out so that they could travel to safety.

An army captain spoke up and asked, "And what is safe? Look around you, son. The world is falling apart. You know very well that we were all here because we didn't believe in the Only. Now look at the book of judgment unfolding in front of our eyes. You think we can just go out there in the middle of all this? How will we survive the extreme temperatures?"

He was right. The temperatures around them were staggering. However, the heat had not affected the waterfall colony. Why was that? Was there a larger force showing preference to one group over the other? The differences would be Knowers or Derogates, believers or unbelievers, those with the incision and those without. What about those who didn't have the incision and didn't believe in the Only? There were too many questions without answers. It was crystal-clear that there was a distinction between that NOVA colony and those outside the walls.

Talique went on, "The Exalter and his followers are deep in the darkness. They have taken on heavy physical afflictions and confusion; they are disoriented. Now is absolutely the perfect time for attack. They will never suspect us to attack a rebel prison. We have the resources. My family made sure of that, and I thank them for their wisdom. You say the temperatures are horrible. Well, we'll just wait until the temperatures out there go down. We may have to go after midnight or in the early morning. I can't predict the future. The risks are secondary. The front of our sights are the people we know who are lost and destined for damnation. Will you forget it when we don't know how much time we have left? Will you stand in judgment, knowing you could have saved a soul destined to hell and rescued them to heaven? How will you answer that to the Only? Will you stay here in safety and comfort when we could rescue someone in torment? Not me; I won't do it. And the holy spirit won't let me do it eithers."

All the men in the room looked down, as if they were all experiencing some form of shame, and they all knew it. They would want rescued if the roles were reveresed. Many people put themselves first when others are in need, until they surrender their heart. They could increase someone's quality of life or even save them for eternity.

The captain said, "All right, I have heard you out, and I don't think a man in this room can disagree. We head out with the hover hawks when the temperature has gone down."

Chapter 49

Shay Lyn and Tyrisha were having a sauna detox session that was lasting well into the night. The heavy brick had insulated them from the heat, until the midday. Now it felt like the heat was sticking. The guards hadn't delivered any chow after bringing their breakfast. The portions they were getting were barely sustainable. They were hungry and couldn't sleep, with their stomachs growling so audibly.

Shay Lynn said, "Oh, this is just getting so rough. I am starting to get a heat rash."

Tyrisha replied, "I know. Me too. Don't worry; I know there is going to be a purpose in all of this. Just keep having faith, Shay Lyn. Come on, let's pray."

They had taken their thin mattresses and put them on the concrete, even though it was lukewarm instead of the usual stone cold. They closed their eyes, lay down, and folded their hands to pray.

"Go ahead, Shay Lyn, you can lead us in prayer. I do it so much, you don't need to hesitate with praying. You have nothing to be embarrassed about; just be honest."

Shay Lyn preferred when Tyrisha prayed because it was easier. She began, "Father, we are so uncomfortable in this heat right now. We don't mind suffering because we know you prove yourself true, and tests help build strong character. But I am telling you being human and suffering physically is the worst. You have been so good to me since my family was taken away. Please help us out of this situation. It looks impossible, and it seems impossible, but I know you can do anything. Please forgive us for any disobedience, and we thank you in your son's name, amen."

Next door, Servantés was working on his west wall, using the small filing device he conjured up. Some ripped bed sheets, a broken pen, and that nail he filed down would be a start for is escape plan. He worked intently on his wall and thought about what he would do when he got out. He would find his family, come back and free Tyrisha and Shay Lyn, and then never lose his family again. It sounded easy, except for what in his mind was tiny interferences such as atmospheric changes mixed with diseases and the other catastrophes.

Servantés was still concentrating on that one spot when suddenly, a sharp dagger end appeared about two inches through the wall right in front of him. The point was staring at him right in the eye. He jumped back and then just stared. The dagger piece that Servantés saw was only the tip of a double pulse sonic round. These rounds went in two phases. First, the round would stick into its target and send a pulse through it. The second wave would eradicate most materials, using a sonic blast that reached a diameter of seven feet, tops. The double pulse sonic round opened up inside the wall and birthed its four spikes into the wall. These spikes helped carry the energy from the sonic pulse. Servantés watched as his wall crumbled with such clearing power and yet not very much noise. It was as if someone sped up time and the stone just crumbled from old age. He was absolutely puzzled. The same thing was going on in the cells next to him, surprising everyone. Tyrisha, however, seemed to expect it.

Outside the prison, a hover hawk was firing sonic rounds at each floor. Holes opened up left to right under each prison window, as the hover hawks glided left to right and began their quick extractions of the weak and malnourished prisoners. The heat was still rising from the hot soil, and the temperatures were still not exactly a pleasant spring day.

Of course, for the NOVA soldiers, the time of extraction multiplied the close to fifteen minutes it took to make a massive getaway. No sensors went off for the prison, so the Knower forces had no idea what was going on. However, toward the end of the extractions, a lazy Circle soldier was sitting in a chair, feeding his face. He had missed the initial blast of the pulse rounds, but something else caught his eye.

Meanwhile, one of the rebels was helping Shay Lynn, who was having trouble escaping. "Come on, ma'am," he encouraged, "we are here to help you. No one is going to hurt you. We are the good guys."

Shay Lynn knew this was surely an answer to prayer, but she was very nervous, even more nervous than the soldiers. As she went to step onto the hover hawk platform, her foot slipped and loosened a rock from the opening on the bottom. The soldiers caught her and helped her in, as the chunk fell. No one thought anything of that chunk because, after all, the pulse rounds had made a lot of debris. However, that lazy Circle soldier had noticed it.

The Circle soldier yelled, "Get the guards outside. Something fishy is going on."

The other Knower replied, "Oh, okay, Gibbs. Get the guards outside? We have a small outfit here, and you are acting like we are gonna defend this rig. Who in the world cares about these smelly prisoners? No one ... and that is exactly why we aren't largely staffed here. You go outside and fight the pointless war."

Gibbs ignored his sarcastic coworker and decided to rev it up and get his gear on. He was the type of guard who thought he could defeat an entire army by himself. He may have been out of his prime, with extra weight to show the lack of his physical activity, but he wanted to give some hurt to someone.

It was done. All the prisoners were in the hover hawks, which began to take off. The hover hawk closest to the ground took off through the tree line. The next one followed. The same thing took place for the other six hover hawks. The hover hawks had two levels, so that prisoners were extracted from the top and bottom floor of a cell block at the same time, without making another sweep. The last hawk was ready to leave and took off. The hawks operated just like a bird, designed with two arms on each side like wings. These were no high-flying jet fighters, but they were perfect for ground extractions and could easily climb to thousands of feet.

As that last hawk was leaving, Silas, the NOVA soldier, saw

something. He was on a mission to prove himself. He knew that he messed up, and since he was an immigrant to the country he felt he had more to prove. He didn't mind. He wasn't going to fake an American accent. He prided himself on who he was. Like the other NOVA soldiers, he wore a special helmet with scanning technology to detect weapons. This special helmet would identify any incoming threats and tell the soldier what to do next. But even though the machines assisted them, they couldn't initiate the actions, which could be fatal.

The scanner quickly zoomed in on the single Knower soldier and identified his weapons. The text descriptions rolled across the binocular's screen.

Silas talked out loud to himself on the rear of the hover hawk: "Unbelievable! This guy has it all."

That was no understatement. Many Knowers put their money down for food, water, or pleasure. Not this Knower. In the past, Gibbs had stocked up and been a survival junky. And after he stockpiled on survival needs, he went for the offensive side of things. That meant arming himself to the teeth. Gibbs had a gravity table that he pulled out; it was filled with miscellaneous weapons hanging in the balance. These weapons sat there, waiting to be picked up and fired.

The Knower started in. He first fired a tracking missile launcher that was heat detected. He threw that launcher down and went for the next. It was an electric disruptor. Like before, he fired it and went to the next weapon, which was a scatter tracker.

Finally, the Knower went for a sniper rifle, hoping if all else failed, he could at least take down a couple of rebels. Silas didn't have time to fear or worry; he had to act. The first missile came, and he fired three widespread torch stars behind the hover hawk. The three mighty blasts ignited behind the hawk at a distance, which displayed heavy fire bursts in the air. As hoped for, the heat missile blew up on the bait. Silas turned the barrel at the end of his battle rifle; he had five different barrels, which fired at different rates. Silas's heart was racing, and he knew these next shots had to be dead on. He knew of only one trick with that he had to stop an electric disruptor blast. If he failed, most likely, the entire hover hawk would lose power and crash, which would most likely kill everyone; and anyone who survived would be executed. There was no doubt about that. He couldn't let that happen.

He fired four shots from his barrel, making small movements to spread the bullets in a box pattern. The four molten shots were filled with falium, a highly magnetic metal. These bullets were not cheap, either. They had their own power cells at the end to keep the metal nice and hot. Once the bullets were released, the shooter detonated the rounds by tapping a button. Silas watched the bullets stream through his lens scanner, and then at the right point, he clicked the button on his rifle with his right thumb, detonating the molten shots. It was a fast paced process indeed.

The explosion spilled out silver liquid that quickly turned solid, forming a vertical wall in the air. The disruptor blast hit the metal wall and fizzled out. But it wasn't over yet. When there is technology to deflect something, another manufacturer will find a way around that loop hole. The shell broke off, and twenty tiny tracker shots continued on to their locked-on target.

Silas quickly hit his ear com and yelled, "Get ready for an EMP blast! I'm gonna use it."

The pilot raised the nose of the hover hawk as fast and hard as he could to take the bird higher. Silas turned a key, and the EMP blast also fizzled out the tracker devices. The EMP blast lost power for approximately sixty five seconds. Those sixty five seconds were no small feat, as the hover hawk was heading down. The pilots tried to hold the controls, and then suddenly, the power went back on just as they were going to bottom out. The pilots adjusted the wings on the hawk and used the under body thrusters to level out. With that danger past, everyone's heartbeats were racing.

Silas still zoomed in, as his defender goggles informed him a bullet was coming in on him, and he knew it was a sniper bullet that had deep penetrating power. There was nothing he had left for something like that. He only had a short second to duck down and brace for an impact. He kneeled down, barely missing a bullet to his head; the bullet went past him and exited the hover hawk, making a hole as big as your fist and hitting an electrical line along the way.

Silas spoke, "We took a straight bullet. Check the electrical systems."

The pilot answered, "I see no digital readings, so I hope we can fly without them. We'll have to just ride this one out."

There were no deaths from that bullet; Silas had thwarted off destruction, and the prisoners were now free. They were all headed to a sanctuary to find rest, peace, and comfort.

Chapter 50

The Exalter sat in his compound; outside were dozens of luxury cars, and inside he had the finest of everything. He had proclaimed himself god and was determined to have the best of everything that earth could offer. He sat on the second floor of his giant mansion and always had staff waiting to serve his every need. Not this time, though. There was no staff around to speak to. The Exalter was sitting in the firelit room, holding a golden cup filled with the finest wine. He sat beside the fireplace to his right, and the large window panels to his left let him view the outside world. It was night, and he could see the distant lights of the city. They were spaced out all over as some building were missing from the destructions.

Something else was missing on this particular night. Usually, the Exalter had several women waiting to have a private audience with him, but tonight, he was in a mood where he needed solitude and a time of reflection. He sat silently, just sipping and then staring out the window and thinking his own private thoughts. He found comfort in all he had done; his mansion was a place of pride. However, it was nothing compared to the temple devoted to him far to the east.

Candon, the Seer, walked into the room and sat in a chair across from the fine leather couch. The fire place reflected off of luxury pieces in the stunning living space.

"Laykeun, you know the river Euphrates is almost completely dried up. What shall we do next, my lord?"

The Exalter stared deeper out the window, concentrating his thoughts. "I will do what I have always done. I will fight and show my power. I am the one who has been down here in this mess, not him. He thinks he is so smart and has written out his plans against me, and then I sit here and watch them come into existence. The end may be written, but I can change it. I changed those who served him; who he thought were so important and… f-a-i-t-h-f-u-l."

The Seer was surprised the Exalter was so calm. Listen, you know I am with you until the end. I am your servant, and I will do whatever you ask. I've been with you this long."

The Exalter's tone sharply changed, as he repeated, "Until the end? There is no end. No matter what, there is no end of our being. I have been here on this dirt longer than these simple minds could understand. I've endured more than they could imagine. I've felt pain that he will never feel. Therefore, I have experienced more than him. I am superior to him.

Before all these people, I had many who looked to me for leadership in a place without such boundaries. It was a prison filled with its own positives, but I have failed to see them anymore in that distance. I don't particularly prefer humans. They are simple, easy, and weak. I have made them stronger for worshiping me. My ways are better. My ways are easy to follow, without guilt or heavy expectations. If I were to have my own heavenly kingdom, my city would triple that of his, and he knows it will anyway. Even with all this destruction, they still look to me to provide, and they still love me. I will show him how weak men are and how his work for them is all in vain. I have built all this, and he will not take it away."

The Exalter reached for his wine bottle and poured himself a full glass. He then reached for another cup and filled that one too. He got up and handed the full glass to the Seer.

After sitting down, and after they both had another sip, he said, "Now, you want to know what to do, and as always, I have the directions to guide you. I am displeased by the prison break where Derogates and other deifiers were actually rescued. I want our best trackers to find them. Someone had to have a chip, and before it was removed, it had to give off the direction where these rebels were going. I want the escapees and the rebels captured to face their punishment. You have three weeks to move all the other prisoners from all prisons to one central location on each continent. On the day I choose, I want them all executed. They will die by my hand and find that wretched pit before they can be saved by anyone. Their fates are mine to control. The world will know that their insolence will no longer be tolerated. I want all forces putting double-time into this."

The Seer said, "Yes, my lord. I will start this evening and work on the planning so that all the Derogates and rebels know there is a god on this earth that demands payment for sins. They have been given their chance for forgiveness and have ignored your mercy. Our followers will praise you for this. As always, you know best, and your wisdom is beyond the ages. I will report to you again tomorrow morning, my lord."

The Exalter finished his drink, rose from the couch, and returned to stare out the window at the city below. He wasn't happy and he hadn't felt the meaning of the word for an unfathomable amount of time. He slowly raised his head and looked straight upward into the sky. His eyebrows came down, and he clenched his jaw, displaying a hateful gaze at the heavens.

$\mathcal{C}$hapter 51

The prisoners formerly under confinement were now free. Sure, the NOVA people had only liberated one prison, but it was something. There were prisons everywhere, all over the world, and others had died trying, while some small successes had been made. The Exalter hadn't put much defense into the prison because he never thought people would try to break them out. Nicolai and Leviticus watched as the people were briefed, and it was all too obvious who the newbies were. They looked around like they were on some type of tourist trip, staring up and down and left to right, taking in the sights for the first time. Fulfilling meals, showers, and an abundance of clean water were enough to make them feel like they could die happy. After all of that mess, they had a new level of thankfulness. Few people ever get to experience what it's like to go from rags to riches. And many people think that refers only to a monetary issue. This issue didn't have even a distant cousin to money. This was about simple basics of safety, nourishment, and hydration.

Leviticus and Nicolai observed all the newcomers. He saw a young brunette walking away from him and thought that she resembled Tyrisha. It made him happy to think of her memory.

Then as the woman turned her head, Leviticus's eyes widened drastically. It couldn't be her. How could it be?

"D-Daddy? Daddy, is that you?"

Tyrisha was filled with excitement as she ran to her beloved father. Leviticus walked slowly, in complete shock. He focused in on her face and saw how his little girl reminded him of Zeneth. He loved both of his little brownies. He thought of beautiful brown-eyed Zeneth as he held his other girl tightly. He picked her up off her feet as the tears overcame him. He wasn't the only one filled with emotion. Nicolai had also been watching this unfold and now realized that the young woman he had given a ride to was Leviticus's daughter.

Outside of those Derogate clothes and all cleaned up, Tyrisha looked absolutely stunning to Nicolai. Not only were his eyes captivated by her face, but it seemed like his heart was in need of her closeness. He wanted to be near to her. He thought how silly he was behaving. He was no little schoolboy, and besides, they were from two different worlds. Why would she want him? He was all mixed up on the wrong side, and she probably would think he was damaged goods. There might be a chance she'd forgive him, but then Nicolai thought he shouldn't get too far ahead of himself. After all, they didn't even know each other.

He thought to himself, *Not yet, anyway.*

Leviticus let Tyrisha down; he no longer felt so alone, and neither did she.

"Sweety, I am so glad to see you. I thought you were gone. Look, I want you to meet my friend, Nicolai. Nicolai, come here and meet my daughter. We have had a small journey together but are pretty much cave pals in here, if you wanna call it that."

Nicolai came over anxiously.

"Dad, I met him already," Tyrisha said. "He gave me a ride home on that rainy day long ago."

"You mean, this is the guy that your mother was so upset about?"

"Yeah, it is."

Leviticus looked puzzled about it all and then thought about where Nicolai and he met. It was back at Leviticus's mud hut in the old black suet village. He didn't bring it up now but saved it for later.

Nicolai stepped in during the awkward pause and said, "Hi, Tyrisha, it's so nice to see you again. Were you saved from that prison? Thank the Only you were rescued from that awful mess. Your dad and I are indeed pals in here. We both seem to think alike, and good company is hard to find. Anyway, I will let you and your dad have some time together. It's really great to see you again."

Every fatherly bone in Leviticus's body wanted to send Nicolai away, so he and Tyrisha could talk. Well, the real reason was so he could make sure there was no connection between the two. Fathers always protected their girls. It was just natural instinct.

Leviticus caught himself, saying, "No, no, Nicolai, join us. Let's go sit down and talk about this and how thankful we can all be for the Only bringing us together. Oh, my little girl, c'mon over here. Isn't she so pretty? Well, don't answer that. We all know she is."

Leviticus gave Tyrisha another hug as he spoke. You could tell that this was indeed Daddy's little girl.

"Wait, Dad, my friend, Shay Lynn, is over there; she should join us. She doesn't have anybody left. I can't exclude her."

Leviticus replied, "Sure, honey, just bring her over."

Shay Lyn had been watching, just like Nicolai, only with different type of mixed emotions. She was happy that Tyrisha had found her father, but she also felt sad that she didn't have anyone to look for her. Her family had passed on. Well, not naturally, but by the hand of savages, and she didn't need to look around for people who weren't there. She also worried that Tyrisha would no longer be like her, now that she had her father. Now she would truly be alone again. She blocked out that thought and went forward, trying to be happy, as she walked over to the trio.

Tyrisha told her father about the vision she had and how she traveled just as the angel had instructed. Leviticus realized now that he did indeed believe she was gone after seeing her clothes on the bed. He knew it all had some purpose. If he had thought she was still alive, he might have done something stupid and gotten himself killed. There were hundreds of thousands of people who had done just that, and their silent bones in the mass graves told no stories. Tyrisha spoke about her journey and finding Shay Lynn and speaking to all the people she found traveling. Some were ex-Knowers or Derogates, and others were just stuck in between. She told of how the Only had protected her and Shay Lynn so many times from countless dangers. She also spoke about the traits that made Shay Lynn who she was: funny stories of being scared in the night by an owl perched in a tree or the awful time at the prison. She claimed that the Only had been in control the whole time. Why else didn't the prisons get destroyed by the asteroids or meteors?

Tyrisha just kept talking a mile a minute: "The Only has protected us, just like he did with the people in his book. He has made distinction between us and those who worship the Exalter. Believers don't have the sores or boils, and you said the rest of the world's water has turned into blood. Look at the streams here on the way in; they are clear. I am telling you, the Only is so magnificent. I am so glad to be here and to see such miracles."

Leviticus filled Tyrisha in on the classes he had taken with Nicolai. They all shared their stories and shared their faith. They were surrounded by a sea of people in that waterfall sanctuary, but to those four, it was just them. It was a time to remember. After talking for hours, Leviticus and Nicolai got up and told the girls they needed to get to bed because they were so tired. They all agreed to see each other in the morning, the Only willing.

Meanwhile, back at Nicolai and Leviticus's quarters, it was finally time. Leviticus was sitting on his bed and started, "So, Nicolai, why exactly did you offer Tyrisha a ride home? You knew it wasn't allowed."

"Yes, I did. I don't know. I just felt like I should offer to take her home. I was crushed from Kiyana's actions and felt such emptiness. I wanted to talk to someone who might understand. I felt led to pick her up. I asked he what it was like to be a Derogate and what marriage meant to her. Tyrisha gave me her idea of marriage, and it sounded so much better than the depression I was living in. I was empty. I won't lie to you and act like right there at that moment, I didn't want to run away with your daughter and start a new life, as crazy and disrespectful as that sounds. She was a breath of fresh air in my polluted world. I have thought about her ever since."

Nicolai looked down, as if he couldn't stand to meet Leviticus's eyes. "Is that why you were snooping around my house in the village?"

"What, that was your house? Oh, well, duh, of course it was." Nicolai tried to explain. "All right, guilty as charged. Oh, man, why did this have to happen to me? I was there, just thinking about everything, and I wondered if she was gone in the great disappearance. I figured she was. Listen, Leviticus, I mean no disrespect, and I will stay away from your daughter. You are my friend, and you are her father. I know what you must think of me from my past and being the evil Knower headmaster with three wives. I get it, so don't worry about anything."

Leviticus gave Nicolai a puzzled look and said, "That man is gone, Nicolai. Your past marriage is over, and so is that life. We don't need to talk about that anymore. When you are a dad, you realize every man out there is human and flawed just like yourself. You still want the impossible perfect man who won't act a dummy like you did but it won't happen. If I could go back in time, I wouldn't have let someone like me pursue my own daughter. It takes time and life experience to flourish into a good man. However, I know a good guy when I see one. You have my approval, but remember, Tyrisha hasn't mentioned anything about you in that nature. All I am saying is, be careful." Leviticus smiled and brought the conversation down in a loving manner as he lowered himself to bed. "Besides, I don't want some stalker creeping out my little angel."

Nicolai laughed and responded, "Well, that won't be me. You know I'm really thankful for how you have treated me through all this. You helped me. I have lived a life feeling so unworthy, and you made me feel like something. It means a lot to me."

Leviticus was proud to talk to Nicolai like that. It is more than a privilege to be kind to someone when they are vulnerable. Leviticus ended the night with, "You just get some shut-eye, Mr. Romance."

Nicolai smiled but had a challenging time drifting off to sleep. He kept bringing up Tyrisha's face in his mind. He dwelled on her features and thought about how kind she was. He thought out scenarios of how they might be together.

The next morning, Nicolai woke up and had a new form of energy to get himself moving.

After showering and cleaning up, Leviticus said, "Hey, good morning. I want you to come on a walk with me real quick."

Leviticus led Nicolai to the southside wing of the waterfall compound. They both entered the large greenhouse. Just like everyone else, they looked up to see the sunlight come through the roof, which spread the growing light over the vast vegetation. The intricate one-way panels on the ceiling let light in only one way; from the outside, no one would be the wiser. The panels looked just like the natural terrain outside, but large examination would reveal an underground greenhouse. The idea was most likely viewed as silly until the people living there grew very thankful for it. They both walked down the long aisle filled with fruit-bearing plants.

Leviticus started, "I want you to know how very special Tyrisha is to me. She is my only daughter, and a man can't know what that means until he is the one saying it. The point is that I feel it is only right that you tell Tyrisha about what happened to her grandmother, June. After all, you were the one who found the real truth. I don't like giving my girl bad news. No father does. I hope you understand."

This was both great news and bad news for Nicolai. The father of a woman he wanted to be with was entrusting him with an important order. On the other hand, he had to tell a sad tale to a woman he didn't want to see hurt.

"Yeah, I can do that. I mean, when the time is right, I can do that, of course. I suppose it does make sense, but June is in heaven, just like the others who went."

Leviticus smiled and handed Nicolai an apple. "You got that right. Why don't you go and give my daughter some company for breakfast?"

Nicolai took that apple and went to find Tyrisha. She was just starting in on a late breakfast after a long night's sleep and was ready for some real food again. Shay Lynn was still in their shared room, so Tyrisha was alone. Nicolai grabbed some cooked steel oats that had been made into freeze-dried gravel candy. He sat down with Tyrisha and cut his apple in half (dicing the halves into little pieces), and then, he put half in his oatmeal. He asked Tyrisha if she would like some, and she, of course, did not turn it down. It had been a long time since she had had fresh fruit.

Tyrisha wanted to know all about what led to Nicolai driving her home that day. He naturally filled her in as they both gave each other their undivided attention. He told her of all the betrayals and how he had not been living the life he wanted to live. He felt like he was eventually on the wrong side. He felt empty. She told of a different life where work was hard, but she was happy. She spoke of how the Knowers she used to work for had all this stuff, but they weren't really happy.

She then told him, "Having stuff doesn't give you purpose. I mean, how can you feel you have purpose if, in reality, you just live for yourself and the stuff you have? It's almost like living for a social status. It just seems dumb to me."

As Nicolai gazed at the beautiful young woman, he was thinking, *I really like talking to her. She is so neat. I want to know everything she thinks.* It got to the point where Nicolai felt like they had built a bond of trust, and he returned to his story and told her how he broke into Cedro's house. He slowly spelled out that this particular Derogate left behind clothes, and they were her grandmother June's. He then comforted her, telling her that she had not been killed and did not have to suffer the loneliness long. He reassured her that June was in heaven. It was already amazing that these two met on different sides, and now this Knower was sharing the Derogate faith with her.

Tyrisha cried and felt her heart move with sympathy for her grandmother; after weeping a while, she regained her composure.

"I love my grandma … You are right. She is in heaven, and that is all that matters. I know I will see her soon. I mean, how many people can say that and know it's true? We are living in such unraveling times, where the Only is showing his power to all of those that thought he wasn't there all this time."

Nicolai agreed, and it seemed like they agreed on pretty much everything. They were laughing and sharing deep thoughts with no hesitation.

Three weeks later, Nicolai proposed to Tyrisha, with Leviticus's permission. They had just spent every day together, and Shay Lynn had also been with them, sharing in friendship. The pair insisted Shay Lynn come along and not stay away. Shay Lynn enjoyed their company and wished for her own knight in shining armor to sweep her off her feet. Many people were happy for the pair, and they often smiled at the young lovers. However, the most thankful person was Nicolai. He was a Knower who stood by and let Derogates receive bad treatment from his past life. He had done things he wasn't proud of. He didn't use to have anyone to talk to about it with. Now, here he was, and the conversion he made was no title name. He wasn't a Derogate, and he was no rebel. He was a normal man who believed in the Only as the true creator.

He was most thankful for the forgiveness factor. The kindness that Leviticus had shown him was more than impressive. It was enough for Nicolai to do anything if Leviticus needed help. The fact is, you cannot repay someone in any monetary value for certain things they do for you in your life. It could be a kind encouragement, provision when you have nothing, or any other kind of help that are a major need. On the other end, another view was sneaking into Nicolai's mind. He had attended the classes and knew what was coming. Even though he knew that heaven would be so great, he still felt somewhat robbed. He wanted the opportunity to provide for Tyrisha. He didn't care if he had to also take care of Leviticus someday. It would be his honor to do that.

Chapter 52

The Circle soldiers in Morgan's unit falcon sweep had piggybacked with another unit and started the rallying of all the prisoners into central locations. There was one location on each continent. The numbers were not as large as one might think for the entire earth. No one was policing the captured rebels, no matter who they pledged their allegiance to. The Circle soldiers thought they were doing the Exalter a service by stopping the heart beats of anyone who opposed him. The only people remaining who didn't follow the Exalter were viewed as worthless. They were more than that; they were a liability and could be killed like animals. Except there wasn't a use for them when they were dead.

Morgan's outfit spent all day transporting load after load from different facilities with people every of language. It was obvious the prisoners knew they weren't being moved to an easier facility with air-conditioning and day spas. After a hard day's work, the five men were together, like usual. They had visited a local bar and then went back to their rooms. They had two large adjoining rooms. After spending nights outside, watching each other's backs and taking shifts, it becomes your new normal. Many of the men had their own opinions from that day. The smell … it was the smell of the prisoners that remained in most of their minds. They were neglected, malnourished, and dirty. It had been a wonder that more of them didn't self-terminate after a week of their harsh life. Every prison had its own way of doing things, and most went unchallenged. Many were tortured so badly they were glad to finally die. Rumors existed of people who had tried to kill themselves and they could not accomplish their own termination. Tales were heard of guns jamming, noose ropes snapping, and survival from high falls.

Morgan went out on the small rectangular balcony, lit a cigarette, and stared out at the view. It was cold outside. The rest of the guys were doing the usual: cleaning their guns, checking their supplies, and in this case, stripping that hotel room of whatever would be useful later on. Used soap bars in the bathroom? Who cares? It was going in their bags for later. It was hard to believe that someone left them there. It is amazing to think back six years ago when things were different.

At that time, it was the middle of huge wave of prosperity, followed by an economic drop-out that will never again be matched. In those days, you would throw out toothpaste when it was too hard to squeeze. Now people would cut that tube open and scrape the base over and over until it was the real definition of empty.

Morgan threw the cigarette butt off the balcony, watching the wind carry it down to the ground. Then he took his pack of cigarettes out of his chest pocket. He looked at them for a second and then tossed them down as well. He went inside and sat down, and then he took out his knife, not bothering to hide what he was doing.

Porter noticed it and called out, "Yo, what is Morgan doing?"

Rodriguez looked over and said, "Morgan, man, whatcha doin'? Put that knife away, man. You acting crazy."

Morgan said, "You know it's easier to be offensive than it is to defend yourself. Think about it." He passed his military knife from his right hand to his left. "The offender has the first strike, sometimes predictable and sometimes not. But if you have to defend yourself, you never know whether you are going to see it coming or not. So you think to yourself and prepare for the worst." After all the peace had been broken and people were reverting to prehistoric behavior form the history books. Morgan continued on, "Prepare for an angry kid with a gun, one of those suicide idiots, or maybe a person like us now in the middle of all this. How can anybody prepare for that?" His voice grew calmer. "You're all idiots. I'm an idiot. I read all this long ago, and still I trick myself. I'm done with it. I'm tired of all this garbage. I'm not goin' down with the rest of the world." With that, he focused his eyes on his right hand as he looked down. "This thing has to come out."

The knife lowered slowly in a strong motion, and he removed the chip like an experienced surgeon. He tossed it on the floor and drew his firearm, with blood trickling down his right hand. Smith and Fields were now in the room, watching this unfold. They could not believe this level-headed guy was losing it. They all thought he was going to blow his head off, right then and there. Morgan lifted the gun out of his holster and pointed it up in the air, next to his head, barrel facing the sky. He then aimed his sights down at that small chip and fired one round into it which was pretty impressive.

Morgan put his sidearm away and was actually talking to the would be dead chip, saying, "You're goin' to hell before I do."

The bullet scattered the little chip into even tinier pieces.

The other men were just puzzled. Morgan went into his bag to start addressing his wound. Smith had loosened his grip on his side piece. He was the only one who thought it could play out a different way, and he would have been ready to take Morgan out if he had to. It was a good thing he didn't have to.

As usual, Smith took his chance to lighten the mood: "Well, great job, hero. How do you expect to get through a checkpoint? You gonna tell 'em a rebel knocked you out and took your chip?"

There had been news reports of rebels actually killing and stealing Knower chips to gather food at ration outposts. However, this idea was flawed. If they went to the more sophisticated checkpoints, then DNA wave machines and even holographic facial displays were used for verification.

Rodriguez grew annoyed and snapped, "Smith, why don't you just shut up, man."

Smith rebutted, "Oh, big boy gonna get your say in?"

Rodriguez stood up, and Porter put his hand on Rodriguez's shoulder to calm him down.

Porter addressed Morgan directly, "Why did you do that? What are you going to do now? You're not leaving us, are you?"

Morgan was wrapping his hand up with some simple field gauze. "Pssssht … we don't even go through checkpoints anymore. Did you guys see any boils or sores on those rebel prisoners today? Oh, you didn't even think to look for that, did you? These chips are evil, and they can lock me up with those people for not having one. You all can try to lock me up if you think you can. I don't really care. I've been on the wrong side, and for a long time at that. I'm done serving the Exalter. He is no god. Look at this mess. He is not in control like he thinks he is. Look at what we are doing."

The men couldn't argue with that. They had killed renegades, most likely innumerable innocent civilians, and now it looked like they were helping with an extermination. No one in that room could return home to their families with pride of some righteous and patriotic mission.

"We have all been so desensitized," Morgan continued. "Look at the people we moved today. I mean, some of them were just shy of being kids. I'm done on this side; it's wrong. I'll tell you all right now: I am changing who I serve. The book I told you about put everything that has taken place on paper. I mean, it predicted the future, which is our present, including the meteors, earthquakes, famines, the sun, the moon, and even the animals. Remember those hawks that attacked us? Since when do hawks attack people and travel in packs? You all are blind, if you don't get it. Judge me how you want. But today, I serve the Only. I choose to believe his son died on the cross for our sins, and it's time for me to do some good. That's right, I said it. I'm not taking the chip, I'm not taking any more orders, and I am not worshiping some wannabe who ain't no god."

As crazy as Morgan was sounding, it was also really making sense.

Smith almost couldn't wait his turn; he said, "Oh great, we got a traitor rebel gone rogue now. What was in that cigarette? Something from the locals? I can't believe you, Morgan."

The rest of the men watched as Morgan got his things together.

Fields said, "He's right, you know? Just look at what has all transpired. I've never seen this book. But I have seen what is going on here. Those rebels didn't have the sores and boils that no one can cure. And they weren't stung by those crazy locusts. C'mon, like they had technology to conjure up some incurable disease. If you take everything we were told to believe from a different angle, you can see things are not right at all. What have these people really done except deny to take the incision and worship the Exalter? I'm gonna take it out too."

"I'm with that, Fields," Porter said.

"Me too," Rodriguez followed.

Smith couldn't believe it. "Oh, wow, guys; is this the part where I get to have the key line and say I'm all in too? You know, I have some emergency candles. I'll light 'em up, bake a cake, and we can have a best buds sleep over party. I'll get the sleeping bags. Later, we can have a pillow fight after we play blood brothers taking out our chips. Sound fun?" Smith smiled and nodded his head up and down in a jokingly manner even though no one gave him a response.

He looked up, breathed in deeply, and exhaled as he shook his head. "I guess if you all are going to make me the traitor, then I have no choice. Mind you, it's because I now tremble in fear for my incredibly valuable life. Plus, I know how Rodriguez wants vengeance on me for all those momma boy jokes. He would most likely be my executioner. Yeah, he would definitely be the one to flip the switch. Yep, it would be him. He's the one. Okay, well, that's settled. Let's all get our knives out and join the cool best friends forever traitor club."

They did take out their knives and removed all those condemning chips. The men were so close in a way that normal citizens would never know. How many co-workers did regular citizens have that had a primary job description of protecting each other's lives? They had bandaged each other up, stitched each other up, and even nursed one another back to good health when needed. It was a bond like brothers, only stronger. Everyone except Morgan wondered what they were going to do now.

Some time went by, and Smith's mental chime told him to say something. "So, ladies, what do we got for the blood brothers plan then?"

Morgan looked at them all and said, "Nothing, the plan is nothing. We are going to keep doing what we have been doing. This way, we remain intact with the regular supplies we need, like food and water. If we are asked to do something we don't like, we'll deal with it then. For now, we need to understand what is going on. Are all these prisoners being rallied to get them into a larger prison or some other purpose? We all know many are being railed across land in train cars. Is that purpose testing, slavery, or even extinction? The plan is to figure out what is going on, and then, we'll have to choose sides."

The men talked about the things that used to make them happy. Porter talked about how he felt better about everything in the path they were taking. He was glad they would stay a group. Smith shared some real comments for once about how he didn't want to feel like he was chained up like a dog. He was tired of not being appreciated and not having a real solid purpose. In these days, there wasn't much purpose at all. Instead, whether it was man or beast, the name of the game was survival.

The Euphrates River had not survived all the devastations. In fact, the river had dried up. It was curious how a blood-filled river could just drain out and vaporize. It was an awful sight, with an indescribably unpleasant scent. The wide river was now filled with dark sections of dried blood. It was an awful sight.

Chapter 53

Everything could not have been whiter. The NOVA people had prepared for everything but didn't count on a wedding. Some women who knew how to sew made a simple dress out of bedsheets and curtains. A walkway was lined with white stones. Imitation cherry blossom trees that were used for decoration were placed around the seating area. Even the chairs they used were white. Nicolai started down the aisle, smiling along with the other residents of the waterfall city.

Nicolai walked alone, and behind him, Leviticus escorted Shay Lynn down the white runway, as Tyrisha's maid of honor. After leaving her at the altar, he walked around the seated group to join Tyrisha at the back. The bride stuck right out because she was the only person wearing white, with her vibrant purple stripe sticking out in contrast. The purple stripe around her waist was very distinguished. Women had hand woven purple ribbon around her white veil, and it looked equally elegant.

Leviticus looked at his little girl and shot a smile at her. "I'm so proud of you, sweety."

She looked at him and tried hard to hold back the tears. "I love you, Daddy," she said.

They walked down the aisle.

Nicolai could only see Tyrisha, despite that large crowd of people.

People were even walking around, going about their business, but he didn't even see them. He was zeroed in on her. What a feeling it was, to think this woman wanted him. He had been through so much dissatisfaction and pain, and he had made many mistakes. But here was this beautiful woman who was ready to accept him and truly liked who he was. It didn't matter that they only knew each other a short time. They both knew, and who cared what people said?

Those people didn't feel the connection, the love, and the unexplained magnetic pull that drew them closer. He watched her as she walked down the aisle. She met his eyes and still fought to hold back her tears. He memorized this moment, and as he looked at her, he couldn't articulate his feelings. He just wanted to be so close to this woman and never let go. The rest of the world didn't seem to matter.

Tyrisha had many of the same feelings. She thought about how thankful she was that the Only had put Nicolai in her life. She rejoiced that she would know love on earth before they all went to heaven. She thought about how kind and comical Nicolai was. She needed his understanding personality to compliment her and make her feel valued and adored. She never knew how needy she was until she needed a man, and that man needed her. After Leviticus escorted his daughter to the front, he did something unusual: Instead of turning around to sit down, he walked to the right of Nicolai and stood beside him. Not only was he the father giving away his own daughter, he was also the best man. How many weddings go like that?

A teacher and fellow believer of the Only led the service. He began, "In these times of harsh judgment and catastrophe, we have two miracles in our presence. The first miracle is of two souls going from lost to saved. The second, these two blessed children have found love with each other and decided to take that love to a step of holy marriage. Outside these walls, the world has polluted the marriage bed in unimaginable ways. The Only tells us that it is not good for a man to be alone. He decided that men needed a helper and indeed we do. This is no one-way street. Marriage is no simple task. Knowing a person intimately and deeply brings a happiness that only those who hold it know. Through such a close and intimate relationship, certain things must be given easily and not reserved. Forgiveness, patience, kindness, and understanding. These two children of the Only have accepted the serious agreement to be faithful to each other and to put the Only first in their union, whether we return to heaven before the day is over or many years from now."

They found it hard to focus on what the teacher was saying. It seemed all their brain power was just going into this moment. They were looking at each other, communicating in the way that only lovers do when they stare deeply into each other's eyes. Leviticus handed Nicolai the ring, which surprised everyone who could see it was metal. A worker had forged the rings from scrap weaponry parts. The ring glistened from the fresh polish, and an elegant spiral design was etched into it.

After Tyrisha said, "I do now and forever," Nicolai slid the ring slowly onto her finger. Likewise, Shay Lynn handed Tyrisha the other ring, and she put it onto Nicolai's finger.

The teacher ended the ceremony, saying, "What the Only has put together, let no man separate. You may kiss the bride, Nicolai."

Nicolai reached gently for Tyrisha's face and lowered his head close to hers. He kissed her once slowly, softly, and lovingly, and then after the release, they both smiled. As they walked down the aisle, people tossed fake flower petals in celebration.

There was no huge wedding cake. Instead, the kitchen workers had a different idea. In a facility dedicated to survival, sugar was not at the top of the list (except for medical supplies like glucose for diabetics). Everyone knew how sick the world was with all the gluttony, drugs, and physical deterioration. The baking crew worked to make thousands of little cupcakes that had different toppings. The toppings were a combination of yogurt and fresh fruit. The display was very neat with red for strawberry, blue for blueberry, yellow for pineapple, and orange for peach. It was a different neat treat for a population that had a lot of the same food over and over. Everyone enjoyed the fruit-frosted cupcakes. After much talking and celebration, the couple was about to go back to Tyrisha and Shay Lynn's room, but Talique came up to them and changed their plans.

"Come with me," he said. "I want you both to have something."

Although they were confused, the couple followed him, and Talique led them to an elevator; using his keycard, he took them the sixth floor, which was the top. He walked to a single door in the hallway and handed Nicolai the key. He opened up the door, and they beheld an amazing, luxurious room. On the ceiling of the bedroom, water was flowing right over a skylight, illuminated by special blue lights for accents. Everything was just incredibly nice and spacious.

Nicolai and Tyrisha kept repeating, "Wow."

Talique told them, "This has been my room because I was the last descendant; it was meant for my family, but they are all gone now, and being all alone in this big quarters can make a man realize how lonely he really is. I want you both to have this place. I want to live with the people here and quit this isolation that only couples need in these times."

Nicolai and Tyrisha thanked Talique profusely. Talique walked out humbly and left the newlyweds. The neat light and the water above was an amazing sight, and even better, it was their place to live. Tyrisha and Nicolai were rejoicing over such a gift, and then, the moment slowed. They drew closer for a hug and the beginning of a more private kiss.

Chapter 54

A large warship plowed through the blood-red sea. Morgan, Porter, Fields, Rodriguez, and Smith were indeed on that boat. They had been selected as among the most trusted military followers of the Exalter. Their mission was to ensure the security of the Exalter when he arrived at a new location.

"All you preppy boys are lucky we didn't have to travel on land. Never would have made it through those checkpoints. But I mean it makes sense. All this pain of war has been hard for me, and that is why we all resolved to self-inflicted cutting," Smith joked with a mocking sad face.

A handful of the men chuckled.

As the falcon sweep leader, Morgan started, "Well, fellas, I don't know what is worse—the unrelenting heat in this giant teakettle or the stench of the bloodbath out there. Either way, we need to be on our toes. I'm in this to win it, men, and I don't care if that means going down, trying to do what's right. Apparently, something big is about to happen, and we are a part of that, for some reason. We need to be sharp. That means wearing your gloves so no one catches on that our chips are gone. I can't tell you our moves until I am briefed at landfall; we'll figure out what to do then. Of course, I am also assuming that the world doesn't explode or something like that before we get there."

These men were working on the inside now. They were all done taking orders, tired of the political jargon that boiled down to some evil power gaining strength and the people becoming enslaved.

Rodriguez said, "You know, I am a little nervous about all this, man. I mean, what are we supposed to do? You think we're gonna take on the Circle soldier army that will be set up around the Exalter? Yeah, right, man, c'mon. You know what it is."

Morgan shook his head and replied, "You know, Rodriguez, if you just listened from the start and quit making up your own endings, things would be easier. We always gotta listen to you bicker like a woman about all the what-ifs. Just take it for what I said. I have a contact that can help us out with some extra firepower. And for what, you ask. I don't even know yet. So instead of trying to be patient while your mind is in a mess, just relax. Think about the things that are important to you. All of us have lost loved ones, and some of us wish we had family that loved us. Just calm down, and the answers will come."

Smith couldn't help himself this time. He extended his arms wide open. "Yeah, Rodriguez, gimme a hug? Come on, man, you'll feel better. Come on … bring it on over. Bring it in, man. No judgment here; let's have it."

Smith was nodding his head up and down while waving both his hands for Rodriguez to come over.

"No way, gringo; go hug the anchor when they let it down if you wanna hug."

The mood was lightened again with chuckles, and all the men sat around, thinking about whatever was most important to them. In the end, it seemed like they were all backtracking and reviewing everything they had done. They had killed Derogates. They had killed rebels. They had killed civilians. They had killed other Knowers because they were ordered to. Each of the groups they killed were important. They were people, real people. The killer may play tough, but he has to think about the opposite. That was, what it was like to be on the other side of those crosshairs. The fact is that it is just plain scary. These men were all rethinking their lives because they all knew that there wasn't much time left. Halfway through the trip, Morgan made sure all the doors were shut, and he began to tell the men stories he could remember from the book that was outlawed. He told them how this was all a part of the story and how he had been in long denial about it all. Morgan also let a lifelong wall down and talked about failures he wish he hadn't had. He even talked about the buried betrayals he had experienced from close family members that he felt every second of every day like a mental disease. As much as he tried to forget, forgive, or even defeat the feelings they were always there.

The men talked for hours, and then, they all agreed that some shut-eye was the next best thing. For some reason, every man could sleep a little better, even if it was so exhaustingly hot.

Chapter 55

Two weeks had passed, and Nicolai and Tyrisha could not have been more in love. Perhaps by chance, Silas, the NOVA soldier, had taken a strong notice to Shay Lynn. The two of them had been getting to know each other better, and yes, they thought about marriage. They weren't going to rush into anything like Nicolai and Tyrisha. They were just doing what they both felt worked for them.

Amongst all the hell on earth, the people at the waterfall sanctuary found peace, forgiveness, and love. Even though they had to isolate and hide themselves from the world, it wasn't bad at all. What can be bad about people surrounding themselves with people they are like? Many had to forgive others, including people who were a part of the Exalter's government. Others had to forgive those who had committed horrible acts against them. Some were robbed, and it is different when someone steals what little you have, not from a house full of valuables.

However, the greatest thing found in the sanctuary was love. Everyone there was kind to each other and worked not for money, not for fame, and not for any other type of selfish gain. The goal was to keep souls out of the eternal lake of fire. The goal was to show the Only's love for all people. His son's voluntary death and resurrection was for the benefit of all humanity. Now people would have no boundaries from the Only, thanks to the son and the gift of the spirit.

A meeting was going to be held in the middle of the sanctuary, and it was a frantic gathering. Alarms were going off with repeated promptings, "Emergency, emergency, everyone report to the middle court."

People were frantic and started feeling that all too normal fear that followed. The fear was who and what might come and do what to who?

Talique got up on a podium and spoke into the mic. "Everyone, quiet down, please," he said, his voice booming through the speakers. "There is not a lot of time. We know that the evil forces of the Exalter are on their way here right now."

The people all gasped, and many women started crying. Standing together in the crowd were the close group of Nicolai, Tyrisha, Leviticus, Shay Lynn, and Silas.

"Everyone, do not be afraid. Isn't that what the Only says in his book? What can man do to us? We have given our lives to the Only. Some of us have rid ourselves of the mark. Some of us have rid ourselves of disbelief. All of us have asked for forgiveness daily, and certainly, we were given it. We have done good work here, starting with a few people and growing to thousands. Look at these accomplishments for our family and how heaven rejoices. These people who are coming to do the devil's work are lost. Were we so different? We will not fight them. We will not kill them, knowing they go into the eternal darkness. My family and I have helped to set up the protection, nourishment, and teaching all of you have received. And that is called love. We will show these hateful people love so they may see. I ask that all of you form a line and grab what you can carry in water and food supplies from the kitchen entrance. We are going to open the waterfall entrance for the last time and walk out to surrender peacefully.

"I ask that all of you offer the gifts of food and water to the Circle soldiers. Do not speak to them; our actions will be louder than our words. Do not fear what happens next. We all think we are in charge of our path, but the Only makes our path. May the Only bless all of you. I love you, and I wait to see you again in his holy kingdom, where all suffering will end."

With that, Talique led by example and walked directly from the podium, as the whole colony watched him. He went to the kitchen entrance, and an attendant loaded him up with a large bag of flour and a container of water. Talique then walked to the giant entrance door. He turned slowly to the guard holding his rifle and nodded his head once, communicating to do it. The guard went through the three-step process of opening the door. He punched in a numeric code and opened a glass plate. Then he typed in a letter code. Lastly, he turned a lever and pulled out a handle. The giant door opened, and Talique stood at the entrance, standing tall with those supplies, waiting as his back was toward his people.

After the shock went away, people were able to muster up some bravery. They joined in and started forming lines with hands full of a supply offering for the hate they would most likely receive. Everyone was saying good-bye and the "I love you," along with crying.

Nicolai looked at Tyrisha and said, "You have no idea how happy you make me. I know what it is to really live and to really love. I know he made you for me. Before you, my life was a nightmare. You have made my life a dream come true. I'm not sure I can stand to be separated from you. I'm so worried for you, not myself."

Tyrisha knew the tears were coming down her cheeks; she replied, "Nicolai, you have been my everything: my partner, my friend, and my lover. Don't you worry about me or yourself. We will be together soon forever. Then no one can ever harm us or separate us. Hold on to that."

Carrying the supplies in their hands, they leaned forward for a kiss and rested their heads gently against each other. Shay Lynn and Silas did the same thing, except they dropped their supplies and embraced in the most meaningful hug either one had ever given. Leviticus just stood and could not focus his thoughts. He watched Tyrisha and Nicolai talking while he followed close behind.

"What if they hurt my girl?" he said to himself. "What will they do to us? When will I see them next? Maybe today, I will go home to see my Zeneth and my mother."

He closed his eyes and pictured Zeneth in their kitchen, washing dishes and laughing as she turned to give him that smile he longed to see after his miserable day at slavery for the Knowers. He also pictured his mother from those childhood memories, where she looked younger and cooked for all of them. Leviticus had disliked it very much to see his parents age. He was comforted in thinking about a place where none of them would ever get old again.

A Circle soldier connected to all the military aircraft began giving the orders: "Listen up, the Exalter wants all these rebels alive. Only terminate them if necessary. I will give further orders as we get closer. We will be the first pod to land and report back. The rest of you, stand by."

The first aircraft went in and zoomed in to see the door opened and lines of people just standing there. This general had been through a lot, and he wasn't afraid of much (or at least he didn't show it).

"They have to know we are coming," he said. "Our intel shows they have sophisticated technology. Land the raven, and I will approach."

The pilot looked over at the general as if he didn't believe what he was hearing. The general looked back and said, "Go ahead and land it; you heard me."

The raven landed, and the general walked up to the entrance of the waterfall, going behind the water and out of sight. The general approached Talique and stood in front of him. He may have been an older man, but he looked like a force to reckon with. His armor was equally impressive. The key point to this man's face was his brown and silver goatee. His military beret also told his rank.

The general started in, "Who's in charge here?"

Talique responded, "You know, we believe the Only to be in charge, sir, but I am the one who has been in control of this facility."

The general wasn't some immature soldier who would have backhanded Talique for using the offensive name of the false god.

"Very well, then. The Exalter has sent us with orders to detain all of you for your idolatry and false worship. In addition, since none of you have the incision, you are also charged with treason by unfaithfulness. Come peaceably, and none of you will be killed here today. Try to resist, and we will not fail in burying this little water hole."

Talique responded, "You have our cooperation, and we all have food, water, and medical supplies that we offer to you and your military."

The general expected cooperation, but this was going too far. He was at a loss for words and just glared at Talique in disbelief. The general touched the uplink by his ear and gave the command, "A full surrender has been given. All ravens land by the river and prepare to be loaded."

Just like that, the NOVA were now prisoners. Massive groups of people were loaded, and more trips were made. No one thought that so many people had survived. It was hard to tell if they people were just lucky or really blessed. And why wasn't this water red? Grids from one inquisitive Knower showed the stream should have been infected. None of them had the sting scars from the locusts or the boils and blisters. Not a single person looked like they had been lacking sleep, food, or water.

It was a puzzling scene to the Circle soldiers. Even more puzzling was when those defiling rebels left the food and water on the ravens when they exited to another large aircraft. One Knower was thirsty and grabbed a water case from a rebel.

After that, he shoved the rebel down to the ground, saying, "Give me that water, you worthless deifier."

The Knower opened a bottle and began hydrating as the rebel was helped up by another NOVA. All the rebels were being flown to Jerusalem, which used to be one of the most violent cities in the world. The Exalter planned a show of force to those who would deny him. He chose an appropriate place filled a false doctrinal history, and that meant Jerusalem. He planned a public broadcasting of massive executions. This would be entertainment for those who still served the Exalter.

Planes landed from all around the world, and mass amounts of weak prisoners were being escorted into lines guarded by military and surrounded with heavy military. Morgan, Smith, Porter, Rodriguez, and Fields had already landed by boat. The group had traveled by convoy and yet still managed to avoid security checkpoints. Earlier that day, they had set themselves away from all the commotion and talked privately in an abandoned house.

Morgan began, "I managed to iron out some wrinkles and get us a whole bunch of Rhino rounds. You boys load these up."

Fields was startled. "Wow, man, I have never even seen these type of rounds before, let alone used them. Everyone says they go through anything and never stick. Guys used to joke and say a Rhino round would go clean through a mountain."

The group was impressed and began loading up the ammunition into their rifles and sidearms.

Morgan continued, "Listen, I know we are outnumbered. I don't know what's going to happen next. All I ask is one last thing: I would like to say a prayer and ask that you all at least listen, even if you don't agree with me. And I'll add I wish you would agree."

No one in the group objected.

Morgan closed his eyes and looked down. "Lord, you know we have done it all: Killed people, you name it, we stole it, and destroyed people's homes and lives. We took out those chips to show you that we choose you. However, one things remains, and that is our verbal and physical pledge; we ask to be adopted into your kingdom. Lord, we come before you and ask you to forgive us for our sins."

Each man thought of all the wrong he had done. At the time, it seemed like they were detached from what they were really doing. Now they felt the emotion of the horrible things they had done. They saw the faces and heard the screams of those they had done horrible things to.

"We choose to believe that your only son Jesus died on the cross for the sins of the world. We accept your gift of the Holy Spirit and ask you to change us and come into our hearts. Thank you for keeping us alive long enough to choose you, even know we didn't deserve it at all. I pray all of these things in Jesus' name, amen."

A couple of the men never felt much emotion, and it wasn't hard to tell a few were holding back tears.

Morgan paused, looked around, and then said, "It's been a real honor being with all of you. I love you all as if you were my real blood brothers, raised with me. I look forward to seeing you all again someday in heaven."

Everyone was pretty silent in respect as the men exited the abandoned house and went to their posts, guarding the prisoners being brought in for execution. There must have been more than a thousand guillotines setup on that large concrete square. People were going to die by the thousands. The group walked up and just surveyed the crowds and the military.

Smith thought it was up to him to lighten the mood: "Hey, guys, since I just joined your cult and all, I was thinking ... How are we going to make a dent in this pig slaughter?"

Everyone looked to Morgan to lead and waited for his answer.

Morgan was ready with his answer; it felt guided by the Only. "We may die today, but this isn't the end. Be brave and remember that. After all, what is there here that would make you want to stay? There is nothing but suffering because of what men like us have done. In heaven, there will be none of this. What will it be like to know true happiness? None of us have known it, so what is that even like?"

The NOVA people were the first in line to be executed. They all had figured out what their fate was. Among the first one hundred were Nicolai, Tyrisha, Leviticus, Shay Lynn, and Silas. The group just stood in line, knowing what was going to happen. Even though every person feared death, as bold as they may pretend to be, this group was also ready to die; that is, if it meant dying for the Only.

Leviticus spoke to Tyrisha and Nicolai, saying, "Tyrisha, you are my little girl all grown up. I am so glad I got to see you blossom into this beautiful woman. Don't worry about never having children. I am more than sure the Only will meet those desires for you two. Nicolai, it has been an honor; you are my true friend and now family member. I am so glad my friend can also be the man joined to my daughter. I love you both. I look forward to what comes next. I love you both." They all hugged each other tightly.

Servantés was at the very back of all the NOVA lines, just thinking his own silent thoughts about his Rosalea and Alejandro. He looked down and closed his eyes to focus intently on those memories. If he was going to die, he wanted to do it thinking about the two greatest things he had in this life. Servantés put his head up and looked around for some reason and had to look twice. His mind took in what he saw a millisecond later, and he turned his head back again. Could it really be? It was ... it was his Rosalea with his child in her arms, and she was crying quietly, clinging onto their Alejandro with her eyes closed.

Servantés looked around and found that the Circle soldiers were just relaxed at that specific moment, and it was like he was invisible to them. He moved backward in line, working so hard to get to his Rosalea. She looked straight ahead with those half-open, tear-filled eyes and spotted her husband. He went to her side and spoke quietly in order to not draw attention.

"Oh, my girl, I am so happy to find you." He squeezed her from the side and kissed her face and forehead. "I thought you and Alejandro were lost forever. I am so thankful to be here with you. My beautiful Rosalea, I love you so much. I wish this wasn't happening."

She looked to her side and up at her tall husband's face. "I was crying not because I am scared to die. I am only scared to die without you. You are my purpose and the only one who knows me. I could love no one more. It is a miracle from the Only that I am seeing you now."

Servantés was puzzled at her referencing. He took up her right hand and could tell. "Rosalea, you took the incision out, didn't you?"

"Yes. When I was taken away with our son to the prison, people would pass and talk about all that was taking place. It felt like I knew it was right all along, and I didn't want to believe it."

"Wait a minute. So you have accepted the Only?"

She looked so beautiful to him as she said, "Yes, we have, and I want you to do the same. I can't bear the thought of you not in heaven with me. Please say you will before it's too late."

"My dear, I already have." Servantés smiled and raised his right hand to show the scar from his own removal. The pair could not have been happier, knowing that this was not the end to their union. It was a moment to be remembered forever.

The NOVA people were all guided along the long wooden stage. Then they were to kneel as the Circle soldiers clamped them into the device. The sharp lifeless killer blade was above and ready to be released to end lives.

Nicolai kneeled down and turned his head to Tyrisha. "You have given me so much without ever giving me a single gift. I can't wait to spend eternity with you."

She began to cry and didn't speak for a few seconds. "I hope in heaven I can show you how much I love you. It just doesn't seem possible here. You are my best friend, and I love you with my whole heart."

Leviticus was quiet because he was ready.

Silas turned to Shay Lynn. "This will be over soon, don't worry. In heaven, I am sure a wedding is much fancier than here on earth. I haven't said this to anyone before. Shay Lynn, I am convinced that I love you."

Shay Lynn cried because she never knew love. Now she knew it, and look at what was going to happen. "I love you too, Silas. You mean so much to me. I just want this part to be over. I really love you."

An aircraft was coming in, bearing the black symbol of the Circle soldier regime. The two Terafin guards exited, and then the Exalter followed. Wherever the Terafins were, everyone knew the Exalter wasn't far behind or in front. He walked slowly and confidently in his fine dress clothing. His long and fancy gray over coat blew in the wind. The Seer also accompanied the Exalter, following close behind him with those unmistakable designer glasses. Across the world, every halovision was broadcasting the scene: Screens everywhere showed those waiting to be executed, with many shots of the waiting guillotines.

Chapter 56

Janae sat on the couch of her lavished home, watching with Boenger and the other wives.

Boenger commented on the programming, "It's about time we get to see all of these stupid traitors killed. Why keep 'em alive in jail? They are such worthless wastes of space. I am bothered just knowing they are breathing the same air as me. Get to it and get 'em killed."

Janae stayed quiet and fought back the urge to roll her eyes. She had been around Boenger and the others long enough to realize she was still unvalued. He could replace her so easily with any girl who was willing to go into a room with the door closed. She fought back those feelings because she was in this for herself. She had to stay in mental control. She had long been blocking out her feelings of wanting to be cherished, wanting to be accepted, and wanting to have some distinguished purpose.

Boenger may have been there to ravage his wives, eat rich foods, and drink sumptuous wine, but Janae had a different story. She was there to feel comfort and to turn her back from the impoverished lifestyle she used to live. She was also convinced that the former Derogates and rebels deserved death. After all, they created so much devastation to the earth that it would take a lifetime to restore it. They tried to use their science to destroy the earth, starve the earth, and even poison the waters. They killed so many people. She hated the Derogates for that. She also hated the poor mud huts and towns. She also hated fighting the idea that maybe she was on the wrong side. After all, her family had been taken in the great disappearance. She fought back the idea that it was the Exalter who took them away.

What if something else happened? Janae lived a lie. She was blocking out everything in order to sustain the lifestyle that met her needs and wants. It was a sad life, but she was willing to settle for it. The saddest part was that it was 100 percent her choice to live in false happiness and true misery. No one was holding a gun to her head.

Chapter 57

The Exalter approached the podium and said, "The time has come to cleanse the earth from these unbelievers. I have been patient for thousands of years. I ended the fighting between all the confused religions, which created such man-made violence. The idea of men killing each other ended when I revealed myself and came into power. What a time of peace that was. And you have had my love for the taking. My demands have not been large. A life serving me is not a heavy burden. It is a life of relaxation and true happiness. Yet there are still people who would worship false gods, denying me. These evil people have used every resource to plague this earth and create destruction. I am not an evil creator; I would never take away free will. So now, instead of taking away free will, I will erase the evil from among us. Today will not be a sad day. This will be a day to celebrate the cleansing of this earth and to finally realize there is only one way to get rid of evil. I want to thank my humble servants and all of my followers. You all will be greatly rewarded in heaven. For these people, their home will be eternal punishment."

The Exalter stepped down off the podium and walked down the stairs, where the Circle soldiers awaited his orders.

A prisoner in line began yelling, "I know who you are. I know who you really are. You created evil. You are that old demon fallen from the sky, cast out of heaven."

At the first sentence, the Terafins began rushing toward the man. Their heavy armor-plated footsteps thudded the hard ground aggressively and their red capes flapped in the wind. All people on the earth had known about the attempted attacks on the Terafins and how they failed. The Terafins could heal from their wounds, and no one had ever seen them bleed. The first Terafin took his scepter and struck the man in the stomach with a heavy blow. The man hunched over, making a sound of breath escaping, "Whoa." The second blow from the scepter went to the man's back, and he fell on his knees. The second Terafin withdrew his large shiny sword. He raised the sword high, ready to behead the man.

Seconds earlier, Morgan spoke into his com, the middle of unfolding events. "I'm ready," he said, aiming down his sights and firing those tough Rhino rounds into the body of the Terafin raising his sword. The bullets plowed through his chest armor, and the second Terafin fell to the ground. The first Terafin went for his side shield, but it was too late. The rest of Morgan's group had already squeezed their triggers. The first Terafin fell to the ground as shots rang out. Everyone was astonished, not so much that the Terafins went down (even though no one thought they could fall). The real surprise was the blood. These Terafins were not supposed to be human, and yet they obviously bled, and everywhere.

The Exalter yelled out into his com device, "Do not fire! Cease-fire at those men."

The group walked slowly forward with their weapons drawn, covering each other from all angles. The Exalter motioned with his hand for them to come forward. The team walked cautiously toward him.

Morgan led the group, and when he was in firing range, he said, "Now, it's your turn."

When he went to squeeze the trigger, the Exalter motioned with his right hand. At the wave of his hand, the weapons flew out of their hands and landed many feet away. They would be dead by the time they tried to make a dash for it. The Terafins began to recuperate; they sat up and returned to their standing position. Their blood stains remained on the ground.

The Exalter glared at the men in anger. "You don't think I see you?

I have always seen all of the false believers. Their false light shines in deceit. I have always worked to destroy them, their lives, and their destiny. I could have killed you all before you even fired. But no, I wanted you to watch all these people die and know you couldn't do anything against my power to stop it. Then you will be the last to die. I am … god!"

With that, the Exalter made the motion to the Circle soldiers to release the lever and drop all the blades on the prisoners. Time seemed to stop after the soldier released the master lever to operate all the guillotines. The blades stopped halfway down, and the clamps broke free on all the prisoners who were bound. The sun shone down in full power, lighting up the sky, as shadows of different objects covered the ground.

Nicolai maneuvered the best he could to look up and what it was. After some focusing in it was obvious. It was the son of God, the king of kings and lord of lords. His golden crown glistened as he and his army stood still for long seconds. The son came closer on his pure white horse, flying out of the clouds. His robe was colored red, as if dipped in blood. His army followed behind him. The riders were draped in fine white linen and also on white horses. The army came closer from the heavens. The king sounded a loud trumpet call. A large angel spoke in front of the king, and the birds of the air obeyed as other angelic beings spread out from the skies in four different directions. Great flocks of the birds attacked the Exalter's followers and the Exalter himself.

Nicolai did what everyone else who wasn't being attacked did: He just watched. A grisly sound was made from the Exalter as he began changing his form. The Seer cowered beside him, trying to cover his face from the attacking birds. The ground opened up beneath him, spewing hot steam and fire, as the Seer fell into the hole, wailing loudly. The ground where the Terafins lay also did the same, as they sunk into the earth, and it closed again.

A beautiful and fearful being descended from the sky. An incredible light surrounded the figure of a large man with white wings. There was no mistaking it. He was an angel. The warrior angel descended from the sky with a large key on his belt and great chains that appeared to glisten in his hands. He also was adorned with armor and a large sword.

The mighty angel bound the Exalter, who tried without success to fight back. Immediately, countless dark shadowy beings appeared on the ground and in the air. They looked like men but were literally alien, with some type of charcoal damaged wings. The dark gray skin, red pupils, and appearance said they had all been in a fire. The ugly beings resisted the countless angels, who threw them into the openings of the billowing earth. This was a cosmic war, where humans were powerless spectators. The earth opened up as the Exalter's followers and military were all cast into the smoking earth holes. The angels covered the globe and were ridding the earth of these ugly creatures.

Then the angel lifted the Exalter into the air and bound him in chains. The angel displayed mighty strength. Meanwhile, the Exalter's entire form had changed, and he no longer looked human. He had started transforming into his real form. It was not a pretty sight. He became just like the other beings. He became like the rest, a gray-skinned creature with tattered and worn coverings. He also had that charred body and charred wings. His pupils glowed red, and where you expected to see the white part of his eyes, it was solid black. His face was the meaning of ugly.

The earth opened just like before, and the angel threw the Exalter into the fiery hole; he yelled on the way down, "Noooo! This isn't over. I will win! I'm more powerful!"

The Exalter had been dethroned, and his true weakness had been exposed. Thankfully, he was gone, for now.

It was time for Jesus to reign, and he fulfilled his promise to return and to bring the eternal peace that all humanity had yearned for. It was time to give glory to the good shepherd, who gave his life for his flock.

All the clamps broke free, and the prisoners to be executed bowed down on their knees to show reverence and worship. Their forms changed and seemed to reflect the very light that Jesus' presence illuminated everywhere. Everyone who was taught the formerly outlawed book knelt to Jesus and worshiped as they gave glory to God. The impressive army drew closer, and so did the king, looking at all of his children, whom he loved so purely. They all remembered the teachings they had received and praised their God. All of those gone before in heaven and earth remembered that they had always looked forward to this day, when the son promised them, "Look, I am coming soon! My reward is with me, and I will give to each person according to what they have done" (Revelation 22:12 NIV).

Finally, their long wait was over. The next step was unexplainable, glorious eternity.

Printed in the United States
By Bookmasters